Usan Rise
of a Merchant

Usan Rise of a Merchant

Kathiresan Ramachanderam

PARTRIDGE

A Penguin Random House Company

Print information available on the last page.

To order additional copies of this book, contact
Partridge India
000 800 10062 62
orders.india@partridgepublishing.com

www.partridgepublishing.com/india

This book is dedicated to Mainyu Athra by Amesha Spenta with all the love and blessings of Ahura Mazda.

USAN

By
Kathiresan Ramachandran

Usan I

"*In the fifth year of his reign, Amesha Spenta, the God King, with tacit approval from the overlord, deemed it necessary to reinstate the office of ascetic spies whose numbers were on the decline. Hawk's Nest embarked on a massive recruitment drive to enlist as many recruits as possible in accordance with the guidelines and the stipulations prescribed in the ancient texts*"

"*The creation of spies in the ascetic order is directed by the high priest after consultation with Amesha Spenta and the overlord. The day to day affairs of these spies is governed by the office of the Amesha Spenta and he remains the sole authority on matters pertaining to the creation and deployment of ascetic spies. All reports are sent to his office in secret and he in turn reported the matter to the overlord in confidence*"

"*It was decreed by Amesha Spenta, the God King, that any person who showed any residue of the "talent" in their person be immediately recruited by Hawk's Nest, trained and thereafter assigned to roles corresponding with their abilities. Suitable candidates, in addition to warriors, included ordinary men and women, orphans and widows. These men and women were made to study various sciences including palmistry, sorcery, prestidigitation, legerdemain and the reading of omens and portents*"

"Selected candidates were assigned to duties suitable to their station and position in life. Those that were recruited as ascetic spies were granted more privileges than others. Widows for example were allowed to be a part of a rival king's harem and they were allowed to frequent the residences of the king's ministers"– Hawk's Nest

———◆◆►◀◆◆———

A millennia and a half had passed since the defeat of the Demon Lord Samsara in the hands of the Tantric Monk Mägi. The taint of the orange sun had been erased and Shamash blazed away once again in full glory, his reign interrupted only by sporadic rain and the changing of seasons. The land however remained dry and drained of succulent moisture. According to most schools it was because the land was defiled by the green blood of demons that had seeped into the porous layers of the earth during the slaughter that was unleashed in the battle between Samsara and Mägi. The hideous face of war remained long after the fighting had abated.

The lotus born Mägi relegated the demons and the unrepentant spirits that once roamed freely in the Betan Plateau back to the abyss but the purification rights had not been adequately performed by his disciples. It was now up to nature to reverse the damage that had been done. Fortunately large patches of fertile green had reappeared and sustainable agriculture was once again an integral part of Betan's economy. The decomposing remains of men and demons provided sufficient nourishment for the land to regenerate.

Areas that were not suitable for farming were filled instead with dwellings and small towns blossomed indiscriminately across the plateau. Some became important trading centers filled with lively boisterous markets and unlike the quaint and picturesque towns of Amestria, towns in the Betan Plateau were larger and attracted a wider range of callers that included among others miners, travelers, soldiers and prospectors.

Usan liked it. Betan had thus far been spared the continuous and relentless battles that plagued its neighboring kingdoms. There were numerous taverns and taprooms scattered across the kingdom and the towns were filled with women who conversed freely and were welcoming in their manner. If the truth be told Usan found the women of Betan to be rather pleasing to the eye.

They were tall, lean and often blessed with prodigious strength. Coupled with their seductive tan, it made them irresistible. He was particularly attracted to their voice which was soft and husky and it sent little tremors through his body. It must have had something to do with their native language which was guttural and rhythmic.

In the five years that had elapsed since his admittance to Hawk's Nest, the bastion of the religious order, he had shot up in height and he was now almost six feet tall. He was slim and lean as he had always been but his shoulders had broadened and he was now more adept at swordplay and archery.

Amesha Spenta had decided that Usan would be more suitable as a spy rather than a warrior and had sent him to

Betan to establish an outpost. It was by no means an easy journey and the road to becoming a master spy was long and often hazardous.

Usan was free to use any means necessary to achieve his objectives. The vaults of Hawk's Nest were always open to suitable propositions and he was at liberty to do as he liked as long as he effectuated the desired outcome.

But if the truth be told the normally fastidious monk had done almost nothing with the exception of setting up a stall at the local market since his arrival. He found his new found freedom exhilarating and with friends in high places he was virtually untouchable as long as he stayed out of trouble.

He rode into town almost three months back, his purse filled to the brim with gold coins, in the company of a couple of pack horses.

He was not clad in the normal loose cotton garments of a monk but in the fittings of a merchant. As soon as he entered the town precinct he made his way to a local establishment, which appealed to his eye.

The tavern was unlike the tavern in Amestria, the only other tavern he had ever been to. It was lively, rambunctious, exuberant, and boisterous. Usan took a step back before he entered the main door and braved the crowd in search of the owner. He made his way to the bar, and was greeted by a young lady an inch or two shorter than him, her hair reaching just below her shoulders. She was pretty and her features were enticing but he set aside any thoughts of fraternity, saving it for another day, and inquired as to the whereabouts of the owner.

The young lady lifted her hand and pointed to a short portly man, his face smooth and clean shaven, the light glistening off his bald head. He personified the typical publican and Usan had no doubts that he would be a pleasant man. Publicans normally were.

His suspicions were confirmed a minute or so later when he walked up to the man whose name was, Norbu and inquired if there were any rooms available. There were, but Norbu insisted that he be paid in advance, which was not an issue of course, given the large sums of money Usan had on him.

That was three months ago and in that time, Usan had stayed in a room on the upper floor of the three storey establishment. It was comfortable and he had a chance to flirt with the barmaid daily, not that he made the slightest impression but that didn't stop him from trying. All in all it worked out rather well for him and he soon became close friends with the owner Norbu and his wife Rinzen.

He didn't do much for the first month; his sense of urgency had deserted him. Maybe it was the plateau or maybe it was because it was the first time that he had been by himself, but he didn't feel motivated to do much and was content to laze around.

The story that he had given the owner and his wife was that he was a merchant from Amestria who had decided to move because of the ominous prospect of war that threatened the once prosperous nation. His store had been razed to the ground during a battle between soldiers and the armies of the Dark Lord, and he was fortunate to escape with his life and his savings. His new found friends were saddened by his plight, and even offered to reduce the rent until Usan got back on his feet but Usan politely refused the offer, though he did say he was grateful for it.

He felt that his misfortune was a result of negative karma, a consequence of bad actions from a past life and he would only be able to repay the karmic debt that was due by starting over from scratch.

Norbu and his wife were taken in by the young man's piousness and instantly moved him to a bigger, more comfortable room without any additional charges. All in all things had worked out rather nicely for him but he had to keep up appearances and thus he went out daily in search of items for the new stall that he had acquired for rent at the local market. He dearly wished that he could have had the barmaid as his assistant but he knew that was merely wishful thinking at this stage.

He met the official who was in charge of the marketplace. Normally it was someone appointed by the king's office. He was a burly looking fellow but amicable nonetheless who immediately refused Usan's request for a stall on the premise that all the stalls were fully occupied and none were available for lease or rent.

Usan flushed out a few gold coins from his pocket, and the man whose name was Chogden suddenly remembered that there was a stall available towards the end of the column. Usan fished out a few more coins and Chogden's memory took a turn for the better. Usan's luck changed in a matter of seconds and Chogden just thought of a stall in the middle section that had been vacated that very morning and was now available for rent. Usan accepted the offer gratefully and after signing the contracts, he returned to the tavern.

On his way back images of another stall flashed before his eyes followed by images of a chain of stalls with his name painted in bold yellow. He was undoubtedly on his way to creating the most extension espionage network in history, surpassing anything that had ever been done before. Hawk's Nest would undoubtedly reward him handsomely.

It was time to celebrate and cider would do perfectly. He had to admit he had a fondness for the drink. He hadn't had a drop in the five years that he had been at Hawk's Nest but endearing memories of the company that he was in, snuck away in a tavern in Amestria, came flooding through. Some grilled mutton chops seasoned with spices and honey would go down well with the cider, he decided.

He sat at a table opposite the bar so that he could get a good look at the barmaid. She must know by now that he had his eye on her. If she did, she didn't seem take any notice. She gave nothing away and let Usan, who was a bit of a dreamer at times, drift away in thought.

He was interrupted by the sound of a dish being placed on the table in front of him followed by a jug of cider. Usan dug away relishing every bite.

He pondered over his little dilemma as he munched through his meal, savoring every morsel. All thoughts of war and Hawk's Nest were suddenly flung far from his mind. He looked up to see the barmaid busying herself with sorting out the mugs.

He had the privilege of taking on an assistant possibly a woman of somewhat questionable scruples, to assist him with his task. The barmaid would be ideal but that shouldn't stop him from looking around either. Despite the undeniable attraction it was only prudent to scout around for other assistants. It was his duty to browse through as many applications as possible. The fate of the known world depended on it.

A prospective employer had the privilege of selecting his staff and despite having a suitable candidate in mind it was wise to sift through a list of candidates to ensure that the most suitable applicant was hired for the position.

He made up his mind to find out more about the quiet, sultry woman who tended to the bar. She appeared to be the ideal seductress. Her features were calm and placid and yet she reflected the aura of a caged lioness.

She had the magnetic pull of someone who was in touch with her feminine side. She was in sync with herself and she didn't need to create an outward public display, which suited his purpose well.

Attraction must be subtle yet profound. The slightest touch must leave a lasting impression, a quality most appropriate for the covert operative. The ideal spy must not just operate on a physical level but on a deeper emotional level that caressed both the mind and the senses.

The cider was slowly going to his head and he began to have vivid visions in his mind. Words were not always a prerequisite and at times the less said the better. Seduction was an art that was perfected over time. The slightest tilt of the head or the toss of the hair said much more than a hundred words could muster.

Words sometimes eroded the moment. Words were restrictive and there were none yet to adequately describe the waves of electricity that shot to every nook and cranny in the body when a person falls in love. Emotions are diminished by words, curtailed by sentences. Despite the inexplicable rush of ardor, Usan was hardly in love.

He turned his thoughts to something else. He looked around at the four walls that were painted a serene limestone white, a color most popular in these parts simply because it was the cheapest to purchase.

The smell of wood and veneer lingered persistently in the tavern and that was a sign that the building was kept in good care and that it was continuously refurbished. It was maintained in a good state of repair. That told him two things, that the tavern was doing well and that the owners knew how to look after the establishment and protect their investment.

He had learnt a bit about investments and returns during his stay at Hawk's Nest. Some knowledge of it was a prerequisite to setting up an outpost. He would have ample opportunity to put his knowledge to good use once he got the stall going. He had made up his mind to venture into garments, especially silk and pottery. In spite of his laid back attitude, he had taken the time to do some research.

Silk production was rampant in rural Betan and it was entirely dependent on human intervention. The best silk in the kingdom came from the Nyama district that was located close to the Betanese side of the Kush Mountains. It was filled with rustic wooden dwellings built from wood obtained from the lush mountain forests that had endured for thousands of years. The Demon Lord Samsara during his reign had kept his demons away from the Kush Mountains fearing the wrath of its guardian. Therefore the vegetation and the trees at the foot of the Mountain continued to flourish unhindered and uninhibited by the black magic of the Dron shamans.

Usan turned his mind to his gracious host and hostess, Norbu and Rinzen. They seemed to be the exact opposite. Norbu was a man with a great sense of humor and a kind heart. Regardless of his weight he managed to get around with ease and had no issues toiling around the tavern keeping his place in good order. His skin was tanned from the continued exposure to the sun, enriched by its luxuriant rays.

He looked like a man who had acquired his assets through hard work. His wife Rinzen was an inch or two shorter than him. Her hair was a rich shade of mahogany and it flowed in waves to adorn her glowing, porcelain like skin. Her eyes, framed by long lashes were a bright emerald green with a spark that seemed to brighten up the world. She appeared to be the picture of perfection, gifted with a smile that would fill the world with contentment.

The pair did not have the good fortune of being blessed with a child and after years of trying they had given up. They had thought of adopting but they never managed to get around to it. Sonum, the barmaid, was like a daughter to them, the child that they never had and like Usan she lived in the tavern, in a room next to the owners.

She said little especially to Usan and he pondered over the tiny detail. Maybe he had made his intentions too obvious or maybe she was being coy or playing hard to get. It was admittedly confusing. Women he decided were difficult to comprehend and he wondered how Norbu had ever managed it.

Sonam had long strawberry blonde hair which was rich in curls. Hers were natural, un-befouled and unpolluted by hair dyes. Unlike some women who had to have their hair done regularly, Sonam was spared the hazards of an arduous task that sometimes weighed heavily on the purse. Her skin was pale, lighter than that of most women from the plateau. It led Usan to believe that her parents must have been from further north. She was probably of Rowinian parentage.

Her features were sharp, flawless and it looked like her face had been chiseled from a single block. Her nose was small and petite. She had thick eyebrows that graced a small forehead and her lips were full and pouty, the color of rose petals.

Her shoulders were broad and slimmed to a petite waist; her breasts were firm and rounded. Around her waist she wore a belt with a scabbard attached to it that held a long broadsword. Closer inspection of the hilt revealed that it was not of local origin and from all appearance it looked like one of those swords that had been forged in the icy fires of Simorg. It was most likely a precious family heirloom that could easily be used with deadly intent.

She had red albino eyes that shined like rare mogok rubies in the light. Usan was unable to ascertain if she was blessed with the talent or otherwise. Normally it would be obvious especially to someone like Usan who was gifted with large quantities of it but for some inexplicable reason Usan was not able to determine her true potential or abilities and that made him uneasy.

She looked up from what she was doing, almost staring him in the face and he immediately turned away. He detected a faint smile and once again turned his thoughts to his stall. In addition to silk, garments and fabrics, Usan had also decided to furnish his store with silverware. Silver was much sought after in these parts especially after the war with the Demon Lord. Its properties were rumored to keep evil at bay and it was valued more than gold.

According to the legend, the lotus born Mägi after he had defeated the Demon Lord Samsara, relegated his consort, the infernal seductress Mara, to a fate worse than death by trapping her in a body that never aged but was un-resistant to the light of day. She is said to roam the Betan Plateau in the dead of the night looking for male victims. Any man who looked into her eyes fell instantly in love with her and she drained the life force, the blood from the veins of her victims to sustain her fragile existence.

The demoness Mara however was repelled by the properties of silver. The strong connection that silver had with the moon and its shinning reflective qualities acted as a deterrent against all creatures with a taste for mortal blood, including the succubus.

The succubus is a female vampire that invades the dreams of its victims. In the dreams the vampire approaches her victims in the shape of an enchanting woman and takes him on an erotic journey. The victim becomes so enamored with the succubus that he slowly drifts away, lost in sexual fantasies in the dead of the night. Each time they meet, the succubus drains a bit of the life away from the victim and absorbs it into her own until finally the victim meets his demise.

All in all silver had a myriad of uses and there was never a lack of demand for articles of silver. Usan even went to the extent of stockpiling a fair bit of silverware in anticipation of a shortage which was bound to occur at some time or other. He had the valuables stored away in the vault of a monastery nearby. When the expected shortage occurred he hoped to increase the prices ever so slightly to add to his profits.

———◆◆◆◆◆———

That was three months ago. In that time he had managed to purchase adequate supplies for his stall. He even had the stall refurbished with the help of local contractors in the hope of having the most attractive stall in the market.

In all fairness Usan attracted a fair few customers because he had a keen eye for products and he was quick to spot quality handiwork. In addition to that he sold his wares at relatively low prices. Prices Usan decided must be proportionate to the local standard of living and profits must be tampered with to make products affordable.

That didn't mean that he did not sell exorbitantly over priced products. To the contrary he did. Certain silk garments for example cost twenty or thirty times the normal price and some silver items were just as expensive. But these were more items of display and rarely attracted any buyers.

He had also managed to secure the services of a young boy no older than fifteen to help him around the stall. The boy's name was Kalden and he was an orphan with the right attitude and temperament. He worked hard, was honest and even doubled up as a guard who slept in the stall after closing hours. Usan of course catered for his meals, attire and all the other bits and bobs that went along with the job.

Kalden was native to the Betan Plateau. His skin was tanned and a stub nose decorated his otherwise smooth face, highlight by a pair of eyes that were an opaque brown. Usan did not detect any residue of the talent in the boy but that didn't mean he wouldn't make a good monk or merchant. It was a matter of bringing up the boy in the right manner and from what he had seen so far Kalden had all the right qualities.

He tried to learn as much as possible about his new apprentice who was most likely going to be his first recruit. From what he had gathered so far the boy was orphaned in a war between two rival factions. His village was reduced to rumble during the bitter fighting and he had lost all his family and friends in the battle.

Usan realized that he couldn't sit around idly forever and that it was time to boost his sales. Three months had lapsed since his arrival and he needed something tangible to include in his report to Amesha Spenta.

The first step in the process was to organize regular shipments between the vendors and his stall. Thus far he was the sole rider who sourced and ferried his products between towns and that slowed his progress. He needed a team of able riders and he was looking for at least three others to be part of his new buoyant outfit. With that in mind he started asking around.

The market manager Chogden looked like a good source who incidentally was now on Usan's payroll. His job was to inform Usan of any new faces that made their way to the market place especially those bearing the coat of arms of the Dark Lord.

So far there was nothing to report with the exception of the stray trader or odd merchant that drifted in. Usan had a little notice put up on both sides of the arch that was the entrance to the marketplace looking for suitable candidates. He had received a few applications but hadn't yet shortlisted anyone. Instead he had decided to kick back and enjoy the trimmings of Betanese hospitality.

Afternoons were the least busiest time of the day. The sizzling heat of the midday sun kept most people away and it was only towards the evenings that the crowd started reappearing.

Usan had worked the times out well. There was the early morning rush to start with which began just after sunrise and the market was filled with people juggling and jostling to purchase their daily needs. The crowd thinned towards the afternoon as the day grew warmer and the sun reached its zenith. The crowd would continue to fizzle and between noon to about four in the evening there were very few customers about.

It was the most relaxed time of the day but workers would continue to pop in and out of the marketplace to grab a quick meal. The crowd picked up again after four and the market would continue to operate until midnight lighted by torches and oil lamps.

The night crowd was a lot more leisurely than the day crowd and the shoppers were much more at ease. These were the people Usan called the prize crowd or the cream of the crop. His best buyers came from this section of the crowd and Usan took additional measures including staying awake to accommodate the crowd that thronged to the marketplace in the evenings and nights.

He managed to get a snooze in the afternoons, glued to his big, posh armchair. At times he snuck off to the tavern to get a little nap. Usan was determined to build a financial empire that rivaled any in existence. It was only that he was a bit slow to get started. Maybe it was a lack of motivation.

It was on one of these hot summer afternoons when he was sitting back on the cozy armchair that he had stuck away behind the counter that a young lady dressed in black walked up to him. He looked up at her and smiled before rushing over to give her a hug.

The young lady had a long bow, primly slung across her shoulders and a quiver of arrows latched to her back. The leather she had on looked like it had been given a fresh coat of paint and it glistened in the rays of the midday sun. Her hair was tied behind her head in a neat knot and she looked dazzling in the blinding light of noon.

Usan could hardly hold back the excitement. "Sister" he cried out as tears of joy formed in his eyes like tiny pearls. It was Karmina, the archeress who like Usan was an orphan. She had managed to find a home with a dance troupe before she was discovered by the God King. Like Usan she too was blessed with the talent and not wanting their abilities to go astray, the pair were taken back to Hawk's Nest, where their talents were harnessed and used for the good of the sect.

"What a pleasant surprise" said Usan. Karmina smiled "likewise little brother" she said calmly. Usan was the youngest of the company that had come together to thwart the emissaries of the Dark Lord in their attempt to usurp Hawk's Nest and everyone had taken to calling him little brother.

"What brings you here?" he asked. "Well I was sent to check on your progress, to make sure you weren't squandering the monies that were given to you" she replied. Usan looked genuinely aggrieved. "Would I do something like that?" Karmina smiled "Given the chance I'm sure you would" Usan giggled and Karmina did the same. "You've been having a grand time, haven't you?" she asked. Usan nodded his head unashamed and unabashed.

They started swapping news, filling each other in on what they had missed, ignoring the people that passed by. Karmina listened patiently as Usan began telling her about the Betan Plateau. She pricked her ears when it came to Sonam. "It looks like you have a crush, if I could call it that, on this girl" she said. Usan faked a puzzled look and Karmina decided to spare him the embarrassment, "that's okay little one" she added smoothly.

Karmina looked around. "Who is your little helper?" She had spotted Kalden lurking in the background. Usan filled her in. Karmina stood up and walked over to the little boy to give him a motherly hug.

The crowd was just beginning to pick up and Karmina decided to walk around the market place just to get a feel for life outside Hawk's Nest. It was markedly different and she did not know what to make of things. It was difficult to readjust after being cut off from mainstream living for five years. She was unused to the relaxed atmosphere and having the time to indulge in the simpler pleasures of life, without feeling the pressures of having to conform. Usan gave her a little pat on the shoulder. "I know the feeling dear sister" he whispered softly in her ear.

Usan II

"*A*scetic spies were allowed to play the role of a priest, a priestess or a wondering mendicant and were required to relay in secret any information that they acquired to the office of Amesha Spenta"

"Ascetic spies were also allowed to assume the roles of mothers, artisans, bards, minstrels, prostitutes or any other role that was deemed appropriate. They conveyed their message to the office of the sect leader through ciphered writing or by means of codes, relaying any information that they gathered to the nearest drop point"

Anyone who is angry, anyone who is greedy, anyone who is alarmed, as well as anyone who disagrees with the religious teachings and the principles of the religious order is categorized as an instrument of the enemy or an enemy agent. It is the task of ascetic spies in disguise, to ascertain the relationship of such persons with each other, with foreign kings and with the emissaries of the Dark Lord"

"The role of the ascetic spy is threefold, to protect the religious order and to expand its reach through religious induction, dissemination of religious literature and religious materials *and to cement its authority wherever and whenever possible."* – Hawk's Nest

On the way back, Usan pondered over the two women, Karmina and Sonum. They were both attractive in their own way but the feelings that he had for each of them was entirely different. Sonum precipitated an influx of emotions that he could not comprehend. The noble institution of spies he decided required the services of both types of women. Mothers and sisters were just as good at loosening tongues as the temptress and the seductress.

"What ails you little brother?" asked Karmina. "Nothing" said Usan silently, preoccupied with the scenes around him. The little conundrum than spun like a weaving wheel in his head did not stop him from looking at all the other gaily dressed women that walked towards the market. This was the best time of the day, and if the rains stayed away, there was nothing better than taking a leisurely stroll to the marketplace.

The city councilors had done a wonderful job. In addition to expanding the size of the market, there were various performances that the patrons could watch at no cost at all in the evenings. Clowns, jugglers, magicians and a host of other artists were on the payroll of the city council to encourage more visitors to come to their city and in the process buy the diverse products that were made or produced in the numerous provinces of Betan. It was clearly evident that Leh was a growing city that would soon be a thriving metropolis.

Without doubt it was the best place to be for an aspiring merchant, especially one with the backing and support of Hawk's Nest. Usan smiled secretly to himself and decided he could make a life of this but he needed able assistants. "Tell me sister, how long do you plan to stay?" he asked. "I am at your disposal Usan" she replied. Usan nodded his head ruefully. Karmina said nothing but smiled discreetly to herself.

The crowd thinned as the pair approached the tavern. Its solid teak walls were elegantly polished and it stood out from afar. Usan led the way to the rear of the establishment where they handed the reins of their horses to the stable hand, Yeshe, who took good care of the animals. Usan had picked him as another possible addition to his network.

They walked towards the wooden door that was located at the rear of the main building. The kitchen was sealed off by a teak panel so visitors who used the services of the stable behind the building would not have to witness the pleasantries of cooking especially those with a weak stomach.

Norbu's cook was a man called Sangmu. He was often seen wielding two meat cleavers one on each hand and Usan could only speculate as to what he did with them. There was however very little sound that emanated from the kitchen and during his entire stay at the tavern, Usan had hardly heard as much as a peep. Whatever he did with the cleavers, it must have been quick and merciful.

They were greeted by Rinzen, who immediately had a room prepared for her new guest, after Usan made the formal introductions. He passed Karmina off as his sister who had come for an indefinite stay to look in on him, which was nothing more than the truth. The pair then made their way to the diners for their evening meal. Needless to say, cider was once again on the cards. Usan and Karmina could not resist its sweet vinegary taste. It brought back fond memories and Usan had a feeling that he would be waking up with a sore head.

They started off with a bowl of Betan Chicken Broth. It was scrumptious and Karmina liked it so much that she immediately asked Rinzen for the recipe. Apparently it wasn't difficult to prepare. The chicken is diced and the meat is separated from the bones. The flesh is soaked in warm water and the residue that rises to the top is filtered and separated from the meaty chunks.

The chicken is then put in a pot together with ginger, garlic, onions, celery, carrots and reddish. Cinnamon, fennel seeds, cloves, peppercorns and salt are added to taste, followed by a pinch of ground coriander and green chilies. The pan is filled with water until it is a couple of inches above the meat before the fire is lighted and the contents are left to simmer for about thirty five minutes. Once it's done, shredded fish is added to the broth. Other ingredients like black pepper are added to taste and the result, a delightful dish of Betan Chicken Broth.

The broth was followed by several servings of lamb mamos fried to a golden brown filled with bits of lamb, peas, carrots and corn. The last dish on the menu was a huge pot of Betan Lamb Curry served with plates of boiled rice.

The pair patiently waded through their meal and in that time Karmina managed to get a good look at Sonum. She doubted that her brother was in love. It was more lust than anything else, but she had to admit that Sonum was a handsome woman. Something about her however kept nagging away in her mind and that night once they had retired to bed she played Sonum's face over and over again in her memory.

Hawk's Nest wasn't the only institution that had spies. She doubted that Sonum was on the payroll of the Dark Lord but there was another institution that had yet to take sides and were equally adamant about protecting their interests - the Alchemic Sisterhood. It was an institution that most people knew little or almost nothing about.

Alchemy was a secret science known only to a select few. It was a combination of matter and spirit, an union between Tiara and Maat. It was far more than the transmutation of one metal to another. It included the infusion of spirits into matter or giving an inanimate object life. Just like the mortal body can be possessed by the spirits of the dead, inanimate objects can also be possessed in similar fashion. The spiritual quality that resides in all inanimate objects is called fravashi and alchemy brings this spiritual component to life.

Between death and the afterlife or the hereafter there is a stage that is known as the transitory stage. During this phase the spirit retains the physical attributes of its former self in a place that is commonly known as the astral world. Spirits can continue to remain in the astral world and progress up the spirit hierarchy if they so desire.

Spirits that insist on remaining in the astral world will acquire the ability to evolve and become spirits with greater strength or higher capacity.

These spirits can be summoned by the alchemist and infused into various articles including trinkets and weapons to make them more potent. The Alchemic Sisterhood is a master of this trade.

Alchemy is a science of unknown proportions and it is a science with reaching consequences. Thus far the Sisterhood has made its teachings available only to its members and kept its secrets within its ranks.

Karmina suspected that like Hawk's Nest the Sisterhood also trained warriors but their ways and methods were virtually unknown. During the Golden Age of the Empire there was an informal alliance with the Sisterhood and there was a mechanism in place to share findings and facilitate an exchange of information but since the demise of the Empire that mechanism had fallen into disuse. It would be in the interest of Hawk's Nest to re-establish, where possible, the communication lines with the Sisterhood in lieu of the fact that both Hawk's Nest and the Sisterhood had a common enemy.

She fell asleep that night with the thought niggling in her head but nonetheless woke up the next morning feeling refreshed. She never felt the aftereffects of having too much cider. She was certain however that Usan would be groggy from the previous night. She had a quick wash, dressed and walked over to Usan's room.

She tapped gently on the door, certain that her little brother would be nursing a sore head and true enough she heard a faint "yes" from within. "It's me" she said softly and Usan replied with a muffled "come in". Karmina turned the doorknob and walked in.

She found Usan in bed, still dressed; it looked like he'd gone to sleep without bothering to change. "Isn't it time to head for the stall?" she asked. Usan lay there silently before crawling out of the covers. The sun was inching up to the midway mark and it was the time of day when traders started stocking the stalls with their wares.

Wagons of fresh meat and produce, some from the previous night would be rolling in packed in ice cubes to stop them from rotting. Farmers would have been out inspecting their animals and milkmaids would have finished milking the cows in neighboring farms. Fresh milk would normally be on the stands between seven and eight in the morning.

Usan had a quick wash and put on a fresh pair of clothes before following his sister out the door. Under normal circumstances he would have taken his time because Kalden was more than up to the task but Karmina made him nervous and he felt that he had to be perfect when she was around. The fact that she was going to remain indefinitely compounded the problem infinitely.

They rode out with Karmina in the lead and Usan lagging behind, disappointed that he was denied the usual scenic tour which allowed him to inspect the women that flocked to the market. Despite not belonging to the noble institution of spies, Karmina was older and age took preference. It suddenly occurred to him that Hawk's Nest may have other spies watching him. It wouldn't surprise him if they did. It was a bit embarrassing to know that his friends were aware of his antics but it was too late and nothing could be done about the matter, not that he planned to change of course.

They went past the main gate that was nothing more than an entrance arch and stuck by the side, on the right pillar, was Usan's notice advertising for suitable riders. The prospective employer stopped for a minute to read his advertisement with pride. It had become a regular habit and Karmina gave him a disapproving shake of the head.

He got suddenly distracted by a passing young lady and the archeress could no longer contain herself. "Ahem" she said, the sound of her voice was slightly louder than normal and he saw the girl smile. The color on Usan's face went up a mite and for a split second it turned red. He dropped his head in feigned resignation. It may have been a signal that he accepted his fate and that he understood that he would no longer be as free as he was.

They rode up to the stall and Kalden had managed to get everything in order. Karmina flushed out a handful of coins from her pocket and handed it to Kalden. "Go get yourself some food and don't come back for at least another hour" she said gently.

Usan looked appalled. His sister actually meant to make him do some work which was rather unbecoming for a young merchant rising to a level of prominence. He was certain that she had willfully demeaned the noble institution of espionage.

Spies he felt had a certain reputation to protect. They were suave, sophisticated men and women who had the ability to make others do their work for them or so he thought. Alas! He was sorely mistaken and his bow totting sister had decided to set things right.

She took over the counter, a mantle that had customarily been occupied by Usan and busied herself with counting the money in the wooden till while Usan was demoted to serving the customers. Admittedly, there was some semblance of old fashioned common sense in the decision because it was Usan that had sourced for the products and he was in a better position to answer any questions customers may have compared to either Karmina or Kalden.

Kalden returned an hour later his belly stuffed with fried mutton ribs dipped in apple sauce and mugs of hot sizzling coffee to find Usan unceremoniously explaining to a prospective buyer why a certain silk fabric was more pricy than the rest. He attempted to hand the change back to Karmina but she wouldn't have it and told him to find a little box where he can keep all his spare or loose change. The boy was touched and Karmina was taken aback by the gratitude that was clearly evident on his face.

They continued in that manner until the afternoon. The archeress found Usan's luxuriously cushioned chair extremely comfortable and Usan was granted the privilege of occupying a wooden stool. Kalden had the honor of sitting on a wooden table in the middle of the stall.

The stalls were uniquely designed. Unlike most stalls which only had the one entrance, these stalls had two entrances, one on either side; the middle portion was used for storage and in the case of Kalden, also to sleep. The stalls at the extreme ends were accessible on one side by a lane and on the other side by a cobbled stone pavement. There were public toilets available for travelers to relive themselves and bathhouses for those who wished to freshen up in the company of some delightful maidens. Usan had made the necessary arrangements with the owner of a respectable bath house to allow Kalden at least two daily visits for a bath and a change of clothes which were kept in a wooden closet reserved for him. He paid the bill monthly to ensure that there was no discontinuity of service.

The stalls were arranged in rows with broad alleys or pathways separating them and therefore despite the crowd there was still ample space to walk around. Ideally there should have been two cashiers one on either side but a shortage of manpower had forced them to have only one counter attended while Kalden manned the blind side and handed any monies derived from sales to either Usan or Karmina.

Towards the afternoon the crowd started thinning again and an hour past midday Karmina handed the counter over to Kalden while she and Usan stepped out for lunch. They walked around until they spotted something they liked.

The food quarter was located towards the extreme end of the market and like the other stalls, the stalls at the food court were neatly aligned side by side and visitors were welcome to choose their favorite meals amidst an assortment of popular Betanese dishes. Usan let Karmina make the selection and she decided on a bowl of Betan Noodle Stew.

She watched as the lady behind the counter prepared the meal. The lady cut up two onions and diced cloves of garlic. She added a few slices of ginger which she had prepared in advance, a couple of tomatoes and chucks of yak meat, followed by paprika and spoonfuls of Betanese brown sauce.

The ingredients were put in a pot and placed on a stove. Water was added to the bowl and a fire was lit allowing the contents to boil. Once the stew started boiling the fire was lowered and the stew was left alone to simmer. The thick broth was then emptied into two separate bowls and served up. Karmina ordered a pot of chrysanthemum tea to go with the meal.

The pair were busy scooping up the contents of their bowl with a wooden spoon when Usan spotted the lovely Sonum doing her usual rounds. The color on his face went up a notch. Karmina who also saw the young lady approaching waved at Sonum inviting her over.

The barmaid responded rather tentatively and flushed the archeress a smile before she started walking towards the table. Usan made way and allowed the young girl to sit beside his sister while he stared blankly into his bowl.

The girls started chatting and soon warmed up to each other. Sonum he discovered was born in the outer reaches of the Empire. He gave himself a silent pat on the back for having deduced the minor piece of information from her looks and the hilt of the sword that she had strapped to her side.

He listened attentively. He slowed down on his meal because he didn't want to be sent back too soon and wanted to remain at the table for as long as he could, for obvious reasons. Sadly he neither played a part nor featured in the conversation.

The ladies continued chatting. The conversation was light hearted and friendly. Usan tried desperately to stop his eyes from straying to places it should not when Karmina suddenly decided to take the bull by the horns and out of the blue, she posed the question, "do you know much about the Alchemic Sisterhood?" she asked. Sonum remained silent and Usan was taken aback by his sister's abrupt manner.

A thousand questions suddenly popped into his head; was Sonum a member of the Sisterhood? .... and if so .... was she trying to lead him into a trap? He wasn't sure of what to make of things and he decided that it was prudent to say nothing and let Karmina do the talking.

The uncomfortable silence continued. Karmina looked directly into Sonum's eye and the barmaid returned her look with an equally steely glare. Usan's hand slowly strayed to the hilt of the sword which he had strapped to his back. It was more instinctive than provocative, an automated response that had been instilled in him at the first sign of trouble.

"Stay out of this little brother" Karmina ordered sensing his move. Usan let out a sigh of relief. Talk about being caught up in impossible situations. This was a true test of courage and he would have rather spent a hundred years meditating in a graveyard in the company of the dead than be asked to take sides in the current situation which looked like it was about to explode.

He watched passively, his eyes moving from one girl to the other when suddenly they jumped off their stools and faced off like two warring panthers. Usan leapt to his feet and slowly stepped back a few paces back, giving the combatants as much room as they needed, not to mention the fact that he didn't want to be struck by a misdirected or mistimed blow, which could prove fatal.

Sonum was the first to react. She drew her sword from its sheath. Karmina was up to the task and she had her bow loaded with an arrow within the blink of an eye, her hands moving at lightning speed. The crowd sensing a fight began to scatter while the braver onlookers formed a circle around the combatants in anticipation of some entertaining bloodletting.

They women eyed each other, Karmina let off a controlled shot formulated more to scare than to injure and Sonum fended the arrow with a twist of her blade striking the oncoming projectile at the right moment deflecting it from its trajectory. The arrow flew into the crowd without doing any damage.

Sonum attacked with a forward thrust and Karmina avoided it with ease. This was getting nowhere and the crowd looked disappointed. They were obviously not going to hurt each other. It was merely a conflict of wills. The crowd booed and jeered disappointed that the much anticipated fight was not going to materialize. Soldiers were on the scene within minutes and the multitude of nosey onlookers were forced to disperse.

Usan decided it was time to defuse the situation. "Can we not sit down and talk about this?" he asked politely, in a manner befitting a merchant. If he thought he had any say in the matter he was sorely mistaken. "Don't you have any work to do" responded Karmina icily. Usan had heard that tone of voice before and he scurried back to the stall as quickly as his legs would carry him.

He returned to find Kalden seated on the cushioned armchair unperturbed by the events that were unfolding. Maybe he just wasn't aware but he looked bored and restless. The sun was blazing away and the extreme heat sapped the energies of most people, Kalden included.

"It's time you went for your lunch Kalden" said Usan handing the boy a few coins. He replaced him on the armchair uncertain of what was happening. Almost half an hour slipped by in which time his heartbeat had increased to twice its normal rate.

He remained seated and stared wildly at the crowd. He wasn't sure which was worse. Worrying about the fate of the women or worrying about his own fate. He continued to churn out a list of possibilities when he saw the two women approaching with their arms around each other's shoulders laughing. What a bit of good fortune; Usan immediately went down on his knees to utter a prayer to the mighty Eryr.

He stood up and walked back to his chair the look of surprise clearly evident on his face. He watched as they walked in and Karmina showed Sonum around the store. After they had finished, she turned to Usan, who had suddenly become engrossed with counting the money in the till. "Sonam is a member of the Alchemic Sisterhood and we have decided to rebuild an age old alliance" she said. Usan merely nodded his head in response. Well so much for his plans of recruiting Sonam as a spy. Still there were plenty of other fish in the sea, he decided, grateful that he hadn't been bested by another spy. Nothing could be more embarrassing.

In the days that followed Sonum rode off to seek the consent of the High Priestess to cement the new found alliance. The task of tending to the bar fell to Norbu who was more than adept at the job than one would have anticipated. Karmina busied herself with the store and Usan went off in search of new recruits. There was a need to make regular trips to the various districts and provinces that he sourced his supplies from.

They decided on a name for the stall, something Usan hadn't thought of in the three months he had been manning it. They called it Usan's Silk and Silver.

It was time to expand and Usan sifted through the various applications that he had received before deciding on who he was going to hire.

There were a few advantages to ensuring regular shipments. It would allow him to widen the variety of products that were on offer and he contemplated carrying fresh produce. It was decided that Kalden would eventually be in charge of the store in Leh. The boy had shown plenty of aptitude.

Usan short listed two men and a woman for the positions; the first was Dorjee who was from the hill tribes that inhabited the foot of the Kush Mountains. He had grown up on a farm and was familiar with the duties of a farm hand. In addition to that he also introduced Usan to a new source of income - yak's milk.

Yak's milk was widely consumed in the Betan Plateau. It had a fragrant scent and tasted sweet even without added sugar. It had a high content of solids and it was usually given to people who were weak or infirm. Its nutritional composition was somewhat equivalent if not higher than cattle milk and it was widely consumed in rural Betan. Usan ran the possibilities in his mind and decided that Yak's milk was a welcome addition to his existing range of products.

Dorjee also looked like the stolid hardworking type, slightly un-kept but Usan didn't take much notice of it. He had turned up unshaven on the three occasions Usan had met him, but Usan was not at all perturbed. To the contrary he would have been very surprised to find a clean shaven, well clothed rider who frequented the country on a daily basis. The man was single so there was no need to worry about regular visits to the family and from all accounts he was honest and trustworthy.

He was of medium height, broad shouldered with a little bulge in the belly, short cropped hair and black beady eyes, all of which were common traits among herdsmen.

His second recruit was a young man called Nawang who had been employed as a scout in the army and upon completion of his contract was seeking the services of a new employer. It was essential that the men were able to defend themselves and the items that they were freighting. Larger traders employed the services of armed men and mercenaries to protect their supplies.

In time, if business continued to prosper and moved in the right direction, it was an avenue that Usan would have to explore. The ongoing war had displaced too many people and some turned to robbery and piracy as a means of subsistence.

Nawang was an essential clog in the mechanism and his ability to spot danger and issue advance warnings gave the company the added advantage of being able to detect enemies and flee when the situation required it.

He was without doubt a military man. Clean shaven and neatly attired, almost impeccable when compared to the other applicants. He had a scar on his cheek, probably made by the blade of a dagger. His hands were constantly searching for the hilt of his sword without prompts or warnings, like he was in the midst of a battle. His skin was weathered and dark, like soft leather that had been left out in the sun for too long. He was charred to the crisp from hours of riding and his body was lean and swarthy.

The third addition to the trio was a girl called Nima. She was tall and slim with fiery red hair. Her skin was the deeper shade of pale and her slight frame was deceptive to the eye. Her baggy clothes hid her muscular body and the beads of perspiration on her forehead made her look like a flower be-speckled by dew in the thin light of dawn. She had deep blue eyes and soft red lips that were almost impossible to resist.

It was a difficult interview to say the least for Usan. He had visions of him stroking her long red hair, casually caressing the soft skin on her shoulders and kissing her lush tender lips. He fought down the impulse and managed to maintain some semblance of dignity during the interview process. Despite her demur appearance he had no doubts in his mind that she was lethal with a sword.

Her hands were a dead giveaway. There were no lines of toil or calluses on them. Instead they appeared soft and smooth like satin which spoke of someone who made her entire living with the sword. She was a hired killer and from the looks of it one of the best in the business.

Together with Nawang, he started mapping out the main routes with backups in case of unexpected contingencies. He also located small towns, inns and taverns where the company could seek shelter in the night or during bad weather. He decided to pay the owners a visit and introduce himself. The lodgings would not only help with his trading operation but might also serve as safe houses when his organization grew bigger.

———◆◆◆◆◆———

During the next few weeks Usan and his company were busy traversing the countryside sourcing for new vendors and suppliers. The first town that he visited was a town called Ghizer. It was an ancient town and most of its inhabitants had moved to either Leh or Gilgit leaving behind the aged and the elderly.

A gust of dry wind drifted through the maze of ancient houses, as they pulled up at the outskirts of town. Wooden cabins dotted the grassy hills and the trees stood tall by the side of the track separating the path from the unpolished homes. The houses were arranged in no particular order and goats were plainly visible, grazing freely on either side of the track, while hens flapped their wings, in search of a meal.

The diminutive appearance of the houses did nothing to betray the wealth that was stored in the farms that were located to the rear of the wooden dwellings. The town produced some of the best silk in the known world and its farms yielded much sought after milk, butter, cheese and eggs. The occupants of this village were wealthy but despite the money that kept pouring in, they treasured their serene unassuming lifestyle.

There was a large tavern that was located at the other end of the track.

As they approached the tavern, they could see ivy and ferns visibly growing through the crevices of the old winding brick path which led to the door flanked by rows of skeletal trees crowned in lemon green. At the entrance just before the door stood a delicate marble fountain and the soft gurgling of the clear water resonated in the surrounding silence.

Usan jumped off his mare and the others followed his lead. It was hardly a fitting ride for a converted warrior priest but merchants did not travel on a war horse and a placid mare suited the purpose better.

He knocked on the door and the aging owner, whose name was Tenzin let them in. After a quick discussion he agreed to provide them with food and shelter whenever it was required and showed them around.

The rooms were well furnished in the mode of the Empire; decorate with old faded tapestry panels with a reddish hue and ormolu furniture.

The curtains were a thick velvet red and hung in generous folds around the mullioned windows lined with thick cotton of deepest plum. The rooms were big but not overly furnished and were pleasant to look at. They agreed on a price and left for the next town.

As they progressed, Usan felt the ripples of ecstasy stream through his body as the warmth of Shamash touched his skin. The birds were active in the sky chirping away as they went in search of a meal and the still clouds lingered blissfully in the air in a chaotic array of white puffy shapes amid a pale blue sky.

Nawang rode in the lead, a few paces away from the rest, his eyes wide open, peering right and left, trying to spot any signs of danger while Dorjee rode beside Usan in the middle with Nima bringing up the rear. The swordswoman traveled a length or so behind the main party and her eyes like that of Nawang were constantly alert.

The towns were a fair distance apart and they approached the next town after a few hours of riding. They traveled without pack horses or mules so there was nothing to hamper their journey.

The next town on the list was Turtuk, a quaint picturesque town set on flat grounds that resembled, in many ways, the towns of Amestria. Tall trees that look like they rised forever lined the track and the lush canopy of green provided much needed cover on an unusually warm day. Green grass grew in tussocks, between the trees flattened occasionally by the surge of unexpected wind, only to spring up as fresh as newly blossomed flowers right after.

Usan III

"It is the duty of the ascetic spy to safeguard all religious rites, rituals and mantras. These should be kept in the utmost secrecy, unknown even to the most devout disciples. Ascetic spies are required to turn the tide in favor of Hawk's Nest through natural or unnatural means"

"Once Amesha Spenta is satisfied that the candidate is suitable, he will dismiss the selected candidate for failing to teach sacred verses to an outcaste person or refusing to officiate in a sacrificial rite undertaken by an outcaste person"

"The aggrieved candidate shall then feign anger and display his contempt towards the God King. Such feigning of anger and contempt shall be done in public for the benefit of an audience that is none the wiser"

"By the completion of their training, the men and women who are selected must be well versed with the sacred texts and with the science of commerce and governance" – Hawk's Nest

———◆◆◈◆◆———

In the space of a month Usan and his team had covered almost the entire Betan Plateau. In all that time Usan hadn't managed a single conversation with Nima. It's not that he didn't try but the girl tactfully avoided him every time he got close. Usan decided he needed to give his approach a makeover. He had to admit he didn't look like a merchant and he might be approaching things with the straight forward air of a warrior priest.

He needed to look more like a businessman. There was a stark contrast between a merchant and a warrior and a greater divide between a merchant and a priest, let alone a merchant, a warrior, a priest and added to the mix was the all-consuming role of a spy. Not that they were particularly difficult roles to play. Usan felt that he was more than up to the task. It was simply a matter of adapting to the right role at the right time.

He had to learn how to shift from one function to the other and do so in the quickest time possible. It occurred to him that he might have to dress for each role. A suave gentleman might impress Nima more than a travelling merchant and as they approached the outskirts of Leh, he decided he would give it one last go before his well-intentioned but sometimes meddling sister Karmina got around to befriending her, in which case all would be lost. He thought of Sonum with regret.

That was all over even before it started. Karmina and Sonum had become firm friends and to make matters worse Sonum was a member of the Alchemic Sisterhood, who had most likely taken on the role of a barmaid to keep an eye on the happenings in Leh. A spy being spied on by another spy, what could be worse? He had to admit he had been outwitted on that score.

No matter he would try his luck again with Nima. It might be an idea to start off with some pleasant conversation. With that in mind he turned his horse and rode up to Nima. "What did you think of the trip so far Nima?" asked Usan trying to sound slightly authoritative, but not too much, because he obviously didn't want to intimidate the young lady, not forgetting the fact that she was a skilled assassin who wouldn't hesitate to slit his throat at the slightest notice.

"It was alright" she replied not taking her eyes off the track for a second. Usan took a moment to think. The problem with Nima was that she never gave anyone a chance to converse with her. He persevered. "I take it that you liked it" he added. "It was fine" was the airy response, in the same tone and in an identical manner and with almost the same answer. Usan gave up. "Good to hear. I'll leave you to it then" he said with a prim nod of the head and rode up to join Dorjee dejected.

"I take it didn't work out then" said Dorjee who was himself the centerpiece of rejection. Usan shook his head. "Ah it's all for the good Usan" said Dorjee rather wisely but Usan failed to see how it was for the good. He was a master spy who had failed twice. It was not good at all. In fact it was a disaster and if it wasn't for his sister Karmina he would still be going down the wrong alley with Sonam.

They rode into town, a couple of hours past noon and were greeted by a handful of people going about their business. A flock of crows pecked away at the crumbs that lay scattered on the ground. The black feathered birds never ceased to amaze him. They fed off almost anything, including carcasses of small rodents, pecking away at the remains. He had watched a crow callously eat away a dead rat once. It was a morbid sight but the bird didn't appear to be put off by the decaying worm infested carcass.

Those were the exact qualities a master spy like him needed - to be able to survive under any and all circumstances. But he needed to do more than just survive. He needed to build his financial empire and he was stumbling at the first stage. Maybe he should try recruiting men instead, they seemed easier to get along with but he had to admit the notion didn't sound too appealing. He turned his head to look at his lackluster companion Dorjee and sorely wished that it was Nima who was riding beside him.

They soon reached the market place and handed the reins of their horses to the stable hand who stood ready in waiting at the entrance of the market before they passed through the arch. Nawang and Nima continued to remain alert. It was like second nature to the pair. Usan took the lead as they walked up to the stall, where they found Kalden and Karmina hard at work. Usan smiled with contentment, the first signs of untold fortunes. He could tell by just looking at the crowd that flocked to his stores. The smile didn't last too long when he realized that the reason was because the already low prices had been dramatically further slashed. His jaw dropped when he saw the revised prices.

When he had recovered sufficiently he took Karmina aside. "Why did you change the prices?" he asked. Karmina gave him a stern look and he knew that he had lost the battle well before it started. "Usan the object is to attract crowds and to build a network". "It is better that we work our way up to being wholesalers rather than continue as stall owners. We need to supply not only to our own stalls but to other stalls as well and therefore we need to keep our prices low so our buyers can make a profit" she continued. "We make our fortunate in numbers not in individual sales". Usan thought it over for a minute and he had to admit that the plan had some merit. On an equally positive note it would give him more time on the road with Nima. He was certain that his sister would have him out again, sourcing for new products and cheaper substitutes in no time.

"I heard from Sonum" Karmina said to liven him up a bit, when they managed to find a quiet moment together. Usan remained silent, unsure of what to expect next. He just let his sister continue. "She will be returning to join us. The Sisterhood approved of our plan to re-forge the old alliance". Usan said nothing, weighing the possibilities in his mind. Now he had two women to content with, in addition to Karmina, Sonam and Nima. He wasn't sure how he was going to cope, but he was confident he'd survive. He was certain that news would get around that he had been flirting with the both of them. Still he couldn't complain. His plan to create a covert organization backed by a financial empire of immense proportions looked like it was panning out rather well.

Karmina had met the rest of his team, he had made the introductions before they got on the way but she hadn't chatted much to them. All that changed during dinner that night. They all had rooms in the same tavern and Karmina was seated beside Nima while he was stuck between Nawang and Dorjee. Half an hour into the meal and Karmina gave him a strange look. There was no need for words. He knew something had been said and his goose was as cooked as the spicy roast chicken that decorated the silver platter on the table. It was all too much. A master spy like him shouldn't have to answer to anyone. He was granted immense power to do as he pleased by the most powerful religious order in the known world. Unfortunately none of it meant much in the presence of his sister. It was time for more cider.

The more he consumed of it the happier he felt. He'll leave the girls to Karmina and continue to pay full attention to building his financial empire. No doubt there'll be other women.

Usan woke up with a heavier head than normal. Maybe it's time to switch drinks, he thought. He decided that he was going to avoid his companions for the day and do a bit of shopping. He dressed in his meager clothes and headed for a large stall towards the rear of the market located close to the food court.

The stall was wedged between two other stalls and was slightly broader in dimensions. It had a fresh sign that was stuck beside the entrance, with the words "Dechen's Clothes Store" painted in bold pink on it. The clothes looked to be neatly arranged in rows sorted out by sizes and designs.

The woman at the till was dressed like any other upper class Batanese. She was casual but smartly dressed. A thin silk jacket covered a lovely white top, and she had on a pair of grey slacks to match. Her face was slightly made up, but not overly done and her long black hair was pulled back in a ponytail. Usan was drawn to her. The all too familiar magnetic attraction came into play once again. There was something in the way she carried herself with a calm sense of self-assuredness that left a lasting impression on him.

She turned her head to look at him and he was struck by how protuberant her eyes really were and the prominence of her cheekbones. He hazel eyes looked directly at him and he was instantly captivated by her charm. He smiled bashfully.

She smiled back in return, her lips barely parting, a faint twinkle in her eye. Usan felt a surge of confidence. He walked up to her and spoke as politely as he could "Good morning ma'am" he said. "I need a set of new clothes". "Is it only a set you need, sir, or could I interest you in some of our latest arrivals that would suit a gentleman such as yourself?" she asked. Usan thought for a moment maybe an additional set or two wouldn't hurt. He had to blend it with Betan's elite after all.

In the thousand or more years that had passed since the Tantric Monk Mägi took the reins of the kingdom, Betan had transformed itself from a plateau that was inhabited by shamans, witches and wizards to become a commercial hub of untold wealth. It had discovered its own unique identity and it had carved itself a niche on the tourist market.

Betan's transformation was influenced not only by Mägi but by the cultural changes that had taken place in the neighboring kingdoms following the demise of the Grand Empire. In the immediate aftermath of the collapse, the kingdoms entered a period that was known as the dark ages.

For about five hundred years, the kingdoms were left to their own devices while Hawk's Nest was recovering from the losses it had sustained following the collapse. Many of the occupants of the former Empire were left defenseless and the once peaceful villages were left with no option but to take up arms to defend their possessions and their loved ones.

Kings and nobles were no longer able to protect the peasants and the feudal system of serfdom became an instrument of tyranny. In the aftermath of the collapse serfs and peasants organized themselves and began to select their leaders as they saw fit. These leaders became known as warlords or voivodes and villages with a voivode became known as voivodeships.

The voivode system that was initially created to defend each village from intruders and marauders in some cases became an instrument of tyranny and many of the villagers, former famers, had taken to being warriors. The feuding and the raids started shortly after the establishment of the voivode system. Some of the voivodes merged with other voivodes. The prospect of war and conquest compelled them to form bigger conglomerates.

The resources of Hawk's Nest were depleted and the religious order had no choice but to form a loose alliance with these voivodes with the understanding that Hawk's Nest was to remain the sole religious order and all matters pertaining to the religion were governed by Hawk's Nest. It was to remain the ultimate authority on all religious matters and in return many of the kingdoms that once formed the union that was the Empire were left to their own devices. The kingdoms were free to adopt their own cultural influences and while many chose to reignite or re-inspire long expired traditions, others like the Kingdom of Betan fused the old with the new to create their own unique blend.

In the years that followed everything changed and each kingdom of the once noble empire had managed to explore its own potential and develop its own cultural traits. The food, the clothes, the cultural performances and even the myths differed from kingdom to kingdom and became as varied and as diverse as the landscape.

Betan like all the other Kingdoms of the Empire had developed its own innate customs and what visitors to the plateau had to understand was that each former kingdom was only united by religion. In the case of the Betan Plateau the prevalent sect was the Tantric Sect that was hugely influence by the teachings of the Demon Slayer Mägi.

Thus far Usan had stuck to the wardrobe that he had inherited from Hawk's Nest with some modifications and alterations to suit the local taste and temperament. It was time for a change. With that in mind he nodded his head. Dechen smiled and took him into the stall and described each item of clothing in detail, giving him an insight to high society living in Betan.

The Betanese elite according to Dechen comprised of "merchants, guildsmen and craftsmen" many of whom had accumulated substantial wealth through their trade. They attended gatherings and formed organizations like the Leh Chamber of Commerce whose president was a member of the Betan Chamber of Commerce and sat on its special committee for new appointees. The Betan Chamber of Commerce decided on, in addition to new member admissions, issues concerning trade in various provinces, including health and safety guidelines and environmental issues.

"The primary task of the Chamber of Commerce was to find new markets" continued Dechen. "It did this by sending trade delegations to neighboring kingdoms and participating in trade shows and other events to stimulate the growth of trade in Betan. The prime focus of the Betan Chamber of Commerce was to increase the volume of exports from Betan and as such it had offices in many of the neighboring kingdoms"

"These offices were staffed by voluntary citizens who invested their time and money in what was generally accepted as a community development program" "In short the Chamber of Commerce was an association of people who worked together to improve the economic and cultural wellbeing of any given area. It functioned through working committees and was staffed by internal members"

Usan digested all that he had heard and the Chamber of Commerce sounded ideal. He ran over the possibilities in his mind and decided that it would suit his needs to have access to all the reports that ferried back and forth from the office of the President of the Chamber of Commerce.

"How does one become the president of this association?" he asked. Dechen was taken aback by the unexpected question. She paused briefly before she continued a slightly surprised look on her face. "Well for starters you have to be admitted into the organization. Admission is done via nomination; you have to be nominated by another member. Business owners with some standing are usually given preference". "How old are you?" she asked. Usan thought quickly and he ran a few numbers in his head. He estimated Dechen's age to be between twenty three and twenty four. "I'm twenty five" he replied. Dechen smiled and that told him he'd made the correct guess.

She held out her hand "I'm Dechen" she said. "Usan took her hand, her grip was firm but soft and he felt his knees weaken by her touch". "I'm Usan" he responded. He continued shopping with the help of Dechen and she picked him out a set of clothes that were fashionable and trendy, but yet reserved, befitting a young up and coming merchant. He had to admit she had good taste in clothes.

Despite their new found friendship, the clothes didn't come cheap and the two jackets, a pair of shirts, two pairs of pants, a pair of shoes and an assortment of accessories cost him almost fifty gold pieces. The clothes were designed by one of Betan's top designers. Dechen assured him that the clothes would make heads turn.

By the time he had selected his clothes and paid for them it was almost noon. The pain in his head had disappeared and just as he was about to leave, she asked him if he would like to go dancing. Usan nodded his head without a moment's thought and then shyly admitted that he didn't know how to dance. "Don't worry" said Dechen, "I'll teach you".

She told him where the dance hall was. Usan realized that he had rode past it on a number of occasions but it never occurred to him to poke his head in and take a look. They agreed to meet at seven unless there was an unexpected shower, the chances of which were extremely rare given the time of year.

Usan grabbed a quick lunch at one of the stalls. He decided on a plate of alur achar or potato salad. It was easy to make and Usan had a passion for potatoes. He chose four well rounded baked potatoes and handed it to the cook. He also ordered a plate of fried mutton to go with it.

The cook took the potatoes and diced it with a cleaver before emptying the chopped potatoes into a bowl. Cooks in this part of the known world had developed an uncanny ability with the cleaver and used it for almost all their cutting and chopping needs. The cook added two tablespoons of sesame seeds to the potatoes followed by a tablespoon of sesame oil. He squeezed half a lemon into the bowl. He then added two cut green chilies, half a teaspoon of turmeric, two tablespoons of ground green coriander and one tablespoon of fenugreek seed. He then mixed the dressing together and the potato salad was ready.

Fried mutton was relatively easy to make. The meat was diced and cut into small cubes before being emptied into a frying pan. Normally two tablespoons of chili powder were added to the dish but it was a matter of taste. Most Betanese preferred their meat spicy. In addition to the chili powder a plate of fried mutton also contained, half a teaspoon of ginger paste, one tablespoon of turmeric powder, cinnamon, cardamom, clove, salt and water. They ingredients were lumped into the pan together with meat and fried for about fifteen minutes. Most of the meat in the stalls was precooked to cut down on preparation time and to ease the customers waiting period. Often customers were hungry and demanded their meal within twenty minutes of placing the order or things could get ugly.

Usan savored his meal, enjoying the quiet time he had to himself. After lunch he returned to his room. There was no sign of his companions but Usan didn't appear too bothered.

Instead he decided to grab a quick snooze so that he would be fresh for the evening.

He got up about quarter past five and slipped into his clothes. He had taken great care in sprucing himself up and by the time he had finished almost forty five minutes later, he was looking like a new man with the outward appearance of a banker dressed for an occasion, somber yet festive. Dechen had without doubt picked out some good clothes in line with his aspirations.

That's what he had lacked so far, someone with a good fashion sense. Karmina, Sonum and Nima were all too preoccupied with the war to be able to appreciate the finer things in life. As a master spy he was entitled to some fringe benefits which he decided to take full advantage of. That fact that he hadn't danced before didn't bother him at all. Merchants he decided weren't expected to be good dancers.

He got astride his brown mare and despite the makeover he decided to stick with the animal. Usan had a fondness for animals, especially the one he was on and children.

Child labor was prevalent in many parts of Betan. Following the Dark Ages, Betan like many other kingdoms of the former Empire went through a period called the Industrial Revolution.

The savagery of war and the aftermath of it, left in its wake nations that were torn to tatters. Buildings, citadels and dwellings were battered to crumbs, torn apart by the turmoil. Most were no longer fit for human occupation. There was an urgent need for labor and demand outstretched supply. In order to satisfy the need, children were employed and in the beginning they were paid the same wages as adults.

But greed reared its ugly head once again and soon their wages were reduced by half. Many were bullied into forced labor. Hawk's Nest had issued a directive that the practice of employing children below the age of eighteen be stamped out but reform was slow to take place.

Despite the valiant efforts of its knights, it hadn't managed to wipe out the practice in its entirety and the growth of industries especially the household sector continued to place a strain on manpower requirements. It fueled the demand for cheaper unskilled labor.

The Chamber of Commerce presented a contemporary avenue to stomp out the practice of employing child labor especially if it chose to disassociate with any member that employed children in its workforce. Usan made a mental note to bring the idea into force once he was elected the President of the Betan Chamber of Commerce.

The ride to the dance hall which was located at the other end of the town was highly uneventful. The sun was slowly beginning to set and the onset of night brought with an influx of people. The town was alive with folks dressed in gaily colored clothes making their way to the market to shop, watch performances and have a meal of their choice. Life in Betan was at times ideal.

It took Usan almost half an hour to reach the dance hall. It wasn't the distance but the fact that he had to navigate through the crowd that thronged the streets that hampered his journey. Avoiding accidents meant that he had to ride slowly.

He managed to reach the dance hall in the nick of time and he saw Dechen waiting for him outside holding the reins of her horse. She was astride a grey stallion that had spots of white on its coat. It was a majestic looking animal that stood almost sixteen hands in height. Dechen had a pink dress on with purple trimmings and her face was touched up with light makeup. Her cheeks glowed and her lips were as red as the petals of a rose.

Her hair was tied neatly behind her head in a knot and her hazel eyes sparkled in the light of the waning moon. The street was lit by torches and it reverberated a nebulous feeling. The dazzling light made her look lovelier than ever.

Usan slowed the tempo down a notch and steadied his horse to a gentle walk. She looked up and saw him approaching. For a brief moment they were lost in time, incapacitated by the moment. He sat there astride his stallion just staring at her.

Almost a minute passed before he gave his mare a gentle nudge with his boot to start her moving again. Dechen saw him coming and she looked up with a smile. "Very smart" she said unabashed. Usan blushed and his face went as red as a beetroot, as it often did, when he was embarrassed. Dechen was the first lady to pay him a compliment. "Thank you" he said politely.

It was plainly evident to anyone who chanced to spy upon the couple that the young lady was in charge and somber gentleman was merely following her lead.

She took him by the hand and led him into the dancehall. "Dance in Betan has been part of our tradition since the Great Lord Mägi, deposed the Demon King Samsara. It was in part an extension of the shamanistic rituals that preceded the coming of the Demon Slayer" she explained. "Shamanic rituals are deeply connected to dance and while they served no practical purpose, the shamans mimicked the near death experience and their ascension up the shaman tree, a prerequisite to becoming a shaman, in the form of a dance".

"These rituals were also accompanied by the sound of drums and the shaman moved to the beat of the drums in fluid motions that was more orchestrated than natural. That did not mean that the shamans were not capable of entering a trance, it merely meant that their actual slipping in and out of the trance state was limited to séances" she added.

"Dances were also performed in worship of the four guardian kings - the Guardian of the East, Mikar Sengge Gochen, the Guardian of the West, Mimar Paggi Gochen, the Guardian of the North, Minag Domgyi Gochen and the Guardian of the South, Mi Ngon Druggi Gochen".

"Each of the four directions was a doorway and during the struggle between the noble King Mägi and the Demon Lord Samsara, these doorways were used by the fallen legions of hell to transport themselves across worlds"

"Anyone wishing to pass through the gates must first obtain the consent of the guardians. During the great battle, both Samsara and the Dakinis who favored Lord Mägi were able to enlist the services of the guardians"

"While festive dances in Betan mimic the shamanic dance of the Dron Shamans, the traditional dances often retold the Epic of Mägi and reenacted every aspect of the battle between the great liberator and the enslaver of all mortals" she concluded.

Usan nodded his head. He was familiar with the history of Betan. It was part of his training. He was required to learn as much as possible about any new territory he was going to before he ventured forward to set up an outpost.

There was a stark contrast between the religious practices before and after the arrival of the Demon Slayer Mägi. Following his triumph over the Demon Lord, Mägi fused the Dron religion, which was the antecedent religion of the people of Betan with the Tantric faith that he preached and promulgated, to create a new religion. The Dron deities continued to be worshipped following the fall of the Demon

King but the mode of worship shifted to resonate peace and goodwill. Dance in these parts was not only related to celebrations but it was also an integral part of worship.

The path to the dance hall was lighted by torches on both sides and the floor was covered with thick red carpets. Dechen took Usan's hand in hers and led him to the dance floor which was filled with people moving to the rhythm of an orchestra. Usan instantly felt out of place and his confidence evaporated within minutes into thin air. He realized how wrong he'd been and merchants were obviously required to have some knowledge of dance.

Fortunately Dechen stepped in to the rescue. "Just follow my lead" she whispered in his ear as she led him to the dance floor. "Start with the left foot" she said. "Take one step forward and bring your right foot to meet it" she continued. "Then take a step back with your right foot and bring your left foot back to meet it" she added.

She then repeated the movement sideways and Usan followed her lead. Within half an hour, they were dancing freely. They continued with the routine until it was almost midnight, when the young lady insisted that she had to be on her way home.

Usan offered to escort her but she refused. "My attendants are waiting for me outside" she said. Usan nodded his head. He hadn't seen any attendants in waiting but he had to admit he wasn't paying all that much attention. He walked her to her horse and true enough there were two burly looking men armed with broad swords waiting for her.

He watched as she got on her horse and rode off. She didn't look like a simple girl who operated a stall in the market but that wasn't uncommon. There were many young women who came from affluent families who operated stalls in the market. It was part of their training and many families in these parts insisted that their children work their way up the ladder.

It was part of their education. While most had attended school and understood the basics, there was some knowledge that could only be gained by practical experience. Usan agreed with this mode of education. It was both practical and applicable to communities that inhabited the Betan Plateau. Its modern history only stretched for slightly more than a thousand years and Betan wasn't as culturally rich as some of the other kingdoms.

Culture could sometimes be an inhibiting factor and it didn't always help matters. In fact in some ways it could hinder social development. Hawk's Nest was much more liberal than many had anticipated and it was its un-rigid approach that had allowed the religion to flourish.

He slept well that night, without the help of his favorite beverage, cider and got dressed as per the norm to join the others at the breakfast table the next morning, eager to catch up on the news. He discarded his new fashionable outfits and used his normal run of the mill tradesmen clothes.

He walked down the staircase and spotted his friends seated around the table enjoying their breakfast engaged in light conversation. He walked up to them and cleared his throat to get their attention. The rest looked up to greet him while Nima looked unperturbed and continued with her meal. His confidence boosted by his exploits the previous night, he sat on the seat beside Nima who continued undistracted.

"Welcome Usan" said Karmina. The young man nodded his head in acknowledgement, beaming with confidence. "I trust you had a good night?" she asked. "I did indeed" he replied. Usan poured himself a mug of coffee and took a sip before turning to Nima. "How are you Nima?" he asked rather smugly. "Fine" she replied in a flat tone. Usan shrugged his shoulders. She obviously needs more work he thought to himself.

"Usan" said Karmina interrupting his thoughts. Usan looked up surprised at her unusual tone of voice. He had a puzzled looked on his face. "I have spoken to Chogden and we'll be taking up another stall" she continued. Usan nodded his head, it made sense, Karmina like him, was keen to expand their business. "I also think that you'd be suited to a more dignified role" she continued. That sounded promising and Usan looked pleased.

Usan found out exactly what Karmina meant by a more dignified role within the next few days. She had him riding up and down the countryside scouring for locations to set up new stores. He was in the company of Nawang and Nima and the trio were put to hard work. In addition to the sword that he normally had fastened to his back, he also put on additional armor and tucked a dagger to the inside of his belt. The locations that they were traveling to were territories that were bandit prone and it was best to take precautions.

Karmina also planned to source for some of their products from the black market so that they could sell at much lower prices and still make a reasonable profit. Usan kicked himself for not thinking of it himself. It was simple yet effective.

He replaced his favorite mare with a sturdier horse bred for hard ridding. The trio traveled light stopping for meals and rest in the taverns they had previously visited.

They saw no sign of trouble, until their journey to Zanskar, a town on the foothills of the Kush Mountains. The road that led to Zanskar was nothing more than a mud track with tall trees and bushes on either side. Zanskar was the largest town in the Betanese sector of the Kush Mountains and it was a major transit point for traders, miners, soldiers, mercenaries and the likes, not excluding of course, the rogues and the bandits.

Produce from all parts of the Kush Mountains were ferried to Zanskar and from there they made their way to other parts of the Betan Plateau.

The desolate track to Zanskar was ideal for ambushes and it was at least a day's hard riding between towns. The trio had the choice of either spending the night by a lonely desolate road or to ride until sunup. They talked it over and decided on the latter. Pitching tents would be too much of an inconvenience and they had plenty of food in store. Hence they decided to rest their horses at regular intervals and continue riding through the night with the aid of the moonlight and torches.

They left Nubra, the last town before they reached Zanskar and planned to arrive just before breakfast. After a hearty meal with lots of black coffee, they packed their tea and dinner, gearing up for a long night's ride. The rode at a steady pace not wanting to push their horses too hard and stopped for breaks at short intervals to give the horses a breather.

It was close to dusk and the hazy orange light of the fading sun lit the sky. Nawang who was riding in the lead casually lifted his right hand slightly. It was a discreet signal. Usan and Nima gripped the reins of their mounts and started to push their horses urging them at a faster tempo.

The initial contingency plan was to outride any ambush. They looked to have been in the clear at first but within minutes they heard the sound of hoof beats to the rear. Fortunately for them it wasn't raining arrows or the trio might have been cut to pieces. Their horses were well rested but so were the mounts of their pursuers, who had been waiting patiently, hidden in the bushes.

They rode as hard as they could for about a quarter of an hour with the bandits hot on their trail. It was soon apparent that they would not be able to outrun them. Usan turned his horse and leapt to the ground, landing on the soles of his feet. He reached for a bow that was strapped to the side of his horse and with mechanical precision loosened the shaft in repetitive fashion. Arrows were whizzing down the mud track in a matter of seconds. Nima and Nawang did the same but preferred to set their bows alight from horseback.

The thuds of falling horses and the loud groans of men struck by arrows soon filled the air but it merely stalled the inevitable. They were unsure of the number of pursuers but it was safe to assume that it would be double their number. At the very best they were looking at two to one odds.

The riders were visible within minutes, clad in black, if for no other reason, then the simple fact that it was the best camouflage for night raids. The sun hadn't yet fully set and the menacing silhouettes were clearly visible by the light of the fading sun, arrows protruding from different parts of their bodies. Usan cast his bow aside and lifted his sword from its sheath in readiness as the injured riders started to swoop down on them.

The riders didn't move as swiftly as one would have expected, the injuries sustained from the arrows no doubt dampened their movements. Nonetheless they kept coming. The lead rider was nothing short of a carcass with three arrows embedded into his body. His leather mail had done little to protect him. The two that followed behind had the odd arrow jutting out of their frames.

Usan who had run ahead of the rest, let the corpse that was the lead rider pass, crouching as he did so to remain out of reach of the weapons of the following pair. The one on the left wielded a spiked mace which was a dreadful weapon to say the least and it did a lot more than just knock some sense into an opponent.

He heard the whiz of an arrow overhead, followed by the sound of broken skin as the arrow struck the rider with the mace, going right through his forehead. He was a goner for sure and Usan ignored him, keeping his eye on the rider on the right.

He waited crouched like a leopard staying low enough to avoid the rider's outstretched sword and as he passed him by, Usan aimed a sweeping cut at his leg, slicing it almost in half. He heard the sudden cry of pain. He jumped aside as soon as he had delivered the deadly stroke to avoid the onslaught of oncoming riders as they passed him by.

Three down three to go. Usan did the same to the last rider turning in time to see Nima and Nawang finish off the other two. The first rider lashed out with a wild stroke at Nima. The swordswoman parried the cut with ease and delivered a stroke of her own which sliced her opponent's jugular. Nawang preferred a more simplistic approach and stuck his sword into the belly of the rider that faced him. The trio left those that were reduced to corpses to the vultures, astride horses that sped off blindly down the track.

They gathered their mounts and rode away without as much as saying a word to each other, wanting to put as much distance between them and the carnage as they could. It was strange but most warriors rarely spoke about a kill after they made it. It was as if they wanted leave the ordeal behind and forget about it as quickly as they could.

They slowed down after half an hour of hard riding. There were no signs of any other bandits and Usan was famished. He reached for a sandwich that he had tucked away in his saddle and began munching on it, his hands still trembling from the battle.

Usan IV

"*The* approved candidate whose status has been demeaned in public is then reduced to the ranks of a humble monk and he or she starts knocking on doors seeking alms"

"The inconspicuous candidate may drift from precinct to precinct, territory to territory, kingdom to kingdom, assuming a posture of religious humility and godly fealty, and in the process learn of plans in the kingdom, within households, within ministers, within the army, in neighboring kingdoms and among wild chiefs, and reporting his or her findings to the office of Amesha Spenta"

"Ascetic spies are granted the power to declare that the gods will be angered and that great misfortune may befall the land in the manner of disease and pestilence, if their instructions and stipulations are not complied with. They may further declare that drought and famine will swarm the villages and wild fires will plague the fields and forests, and torrential rain will cause unrelenting floods if an unfriendly monarch continues to reign and instigate neighbors and tribesmen to depose or dispose of their king or leader."

"These spies may promise riches beyond belief and power beyond measure. They may promise that the gods will look favorably *on any rebel who stands against an enemy king and reward him generously. They may promise them a plot of land of their own, and that all wealth and land confiscated from the king and his kindred will be divided equally among the rebel army" - Hawk's Nest*

⟡

They reached Zanskar well before sun-up, bruised but otherwise in good order and made their way to a local inn. The streets were empty in the early hours before dawn with the exception of the odd street dog yelping away.

Nawang made a gesture with his hand but the dog took no notice. It continued its incessant barking. It's slobbering and panting releasing puffs of white smog in the cold morning air. Despite the warm days, the nights in Zanskar were sometimes unbearably cold. The high altitude and a lack of cloud cover allowed the heat to dissipate quickly after sunset only to be replaced by the daunting coldness of the night.

Usan threw the remains of his sandwich at the dog and it wagged its tail scampering on all fours to devour what looked like its morning breakfast. It may come as a surprise to many but dogs in these parts had an appetite for bread and vegetables. Many dog owners were vegetarians and they choose to raise their pets in the same manner.

In Southern Rowina, which was separated from the Betan Plateau by the Kush Mountains, respect for dogs was a principle of the prevailing religion. The dog is praised for its loyalty, its intelligence and is accorded special spiritual virtues.

A dog's gaze is considered to be purifying and it drives off Nasü or the rot demon. A dog is often brought in the presence of the dead so that it can cast its sight on the spirit as it leaves the body and keep evil at bay.

There are various spiritual benefits that are obtained from this ceremony. The dog's two dimensional vision can spot any malicious spirits that might linger around the body of the deceased. If the dog remains silent, then the omens are good and that means that there are no malevolent spirits in the vicinity to lead the spirit of the deceased astray. However if the dog howls it means that there are evil spirits lurking in the vicinity and that the family of the deceased must turn to reciting verses from the sacred texts to keep the evil at bay so that the spirit of the deceased isn't led astray.

They reached the inn that was located on the outskirts of town, sufficiently recovered from their midnight escapade. Usan banged on the doors as hard as he could. He knew the owner having met him on a previous visit and a few hard pounds later, he heard the sound of the door being unlatched from inside.

They left their horses hitched to a post and tumbled in visibly tired from the ride and instantly requested for three rooms which were readily available. They made their way to the rooms after finishing off a large bowl of Betan Stew that was left over from the previous day, scooping it up with thin wooden spoons.

There were three standard ingredients to a bowl of Betan Stew - boneless chicken, boneless mutton and potatoes. Other ingredients may include carrots, salt, peanut oil, minced garlic, coarsely ground salary seeds, scallions, black pepper, butter, ginger, coriander and cumin - all of which were put in a bowl, blended together and boiled. It was by far an appetizing meal that was easy to prepare.

They made their way to the sparsely decorated rooms, which were rarely refurbished because of the quality of guests that the inn attracted. Most of its frequenters were miners who traveled through town to peddle nuggets that they had mined in the rich alluvial veins and rivers close to the Kush Mountains.

Many of the merchants and tradesmen stayed in a hotel aptly named the "Tradesman". It was a much more luxuriant enterprise than the modest inn that they occupied but given the early hour, Usan felt it was inappropriate to trouble the owners. It was highly unlikely that they were open for business at that time of day. Zanskar was a town that went to sleep after midnight and didn't rise until dawn. In addition to that the trio were too tired to prolong their journey any further.

The slept through the morning and regrouped at midday fresh and newly attired for lunch to discuss their plans. Nothing was said about the events that had transpired the night before and a faint flicker of hope came to light in Usan's heart. Nima might now look at him as a shining hero, someone who was valiant and brave and who didn't falter at the first sign of trouble but sadly he was disappointed yet again. She remained silent, calm and composed as per her normal self.

She was without doubt an assassin and unlike the assassins from Hawk's Nest who he was familiar with, she had a touch of steel in her exterior that was almost impossible to breakdown. From what he had gathered so far, the information courtesy of Karmina his sister, she had grown up in the mines of Tarchem - a lonely desolate kingdom, in the unchartered regions, where mining was the prime occupation.

The slave trade was rampant in the unchartered regions and the ongoing war between the Dark Lord and Hawk's Nest prevented intervention from either side because the mineral wealth that was shipped out from the mines were essential to both sides to fuel their respective war machines.

The mines of Tarchem extended well into the ground and many of the subterranean caves that were rich in mineral deposits were partly converted into dwellings by miners and their families who were freed from the binds of slavery after years of service.

Slaves are required to serve for a minimum of twelve years before they are granted their freedom. Children were only allowed to remain with their parents until the age of eighteen. Between the ages of eighteen to thirty the slave children were the property of the crown and were employed in the mines of Tarchem. Those that were extremely fortunate were absorbed into the army. Those that were sick or too infirm to work in the mines were put to a quick and merciful death.

Tarchem assassins unlike those from Hawk's Nest were not from the military. Assassins were recruited from the families of those that had survived the hell pits of Tarchem. "Hell pits" was a name given to the colossal arenas that were scattered across the kingdom. There were close to a hundred arenas in Tarchem. The largest was located in the capital Gishu and seated over one hundred thousand spectators at a time. The mammoth structure took almost twenty years to build and hundreds of slaves died in the process, many crushed to death by falling stones.

Assassins started out as gladiators and they were selected from the ranks of children who displayed a greater affinity to the Sky God Anu and his consort Innana than others. Anu is the patron god of Tarchem and his wife Innana, the goddess of fertility, love and war is the patron goddess. The fury of Anu and the passion of Innana was a deadly combination and it produced the most lethal assassins. Sexy, sultry and filled with eroticism, Tarchem assassins were reputed to be the most lethal in the world and were only selected from the ranks of women. According to the ancient seers of Tarchem, the Anu - Innana combination would not favor men. Males were used only as sparing partners and were not allowed to progress on as gladiators.

Tarchem assassins instilled fear in the hearts of all men. Innana is the rightful matriarch of these sophisticated women because she bore the first race of assassins and she continues to do so every spring. She enters each year, at the time of early spring into wedlock with Anu and the couple consummated their marriage annually. As a result she becomes pregnant and rejuvenates the race of assassins. To be selected as a Tarchem assassin it is a prerequisite that the child be conceived in spring. These children have a closer affinity to Anu and Innana than any other children.

This reproduction of life is partly described as the resurrection. The actual wedding takes place in the netherworld, in Irkalla, which is located deep within a subterranean cave, in a temple called the palace of the gods, and is witnessed by all the gods in heaven. Up to the time of the vernal equinox Innana remains a virgin appearing in the heavens as Virgo. With the onset of the equinox the virgin becomes a mother, the sole creatrix and the bearer of all assassins revealing herself in the heavens as a sublime lady who holds a baby in her arms which she nourishes with her breasts.

The temple of Anu and Innana is called the Temple of Kham and its priestesses are gifted with the ability to foretell the future or clairvoyance. The first High Priestess of the Temple of Kham was Emeshe, the daughter of Anu and Innana, the primordial assassin. She is eternal.

The High Priestess presides over all religious ceremonies dedicated to Anu and Innana and during these sacred rites libations are offered to the Gods and Goddesses. An excerpt from the private journals of the first High Priestess reads as follows: - "I made a sacrifice to the gods, and poured out libations from the mountain top. Seven cauldrons I set upon stands and into them I heaped wood, cane, cedar and myrtle. When the gods inhaled the sweet fragrance they gathered like sheep to savor the sweet sacrifice".

Upon completion of their pupilage in the Temple of Kham, the girls were sent to the hell pits of Tarchem and there they acquired their skills with a blade under the guidance and tutelage of master gladiators whose hair is dyed red to reflect the rage and fury of Nergal, the God of War and the patron deity of Gishu. They are then initiated into the order of gladiators and taught to use all manner of weapons.

It was a difficult proposition for Usan, a tossup between the sensual aura of Nima and the qualities of the more subservient Dechen. Maybe he had been fortunate in life and the mighty Eryr had decreed for him to have three consorts - Sonum, Nima and Dechen. The thought appealed to him.

He was brought back abruptly to the land of the living by the deep unmistakable male voice of Nawang, "what are you having for lunch?" he asked and the dream came to an abrupt end, at least temporarily anyway. He thought for a moment and ordered a plate of fried mutton and white rice.

He was munching through his meal, lost deep in thought when he turned his head towards Nima and asked "What is gladiator training like?" She paused before she answered. "I liked it" she said. "You had to become adept at various swords and different types of weapons".

"There are two types of gladiators, light gladiators and heavy gladiators. Light gladiators fought in the style of a fisherman. They wore light armor, without a helmet or a shield, much like you're dressed now, in a leather mail shirt and a sword, only theirs is strapped to the side"

"Light armor gives the gladiator the ability to move with speed and take evasive measures when the need arises. In the arena these gladiators fight with a fisherman's net and a trident, and hope to entangle their opponents, moving around them in circles"

"The heavily armored gladiator on the other hand is equipped with breastplates, a shield and fitted with leather greaves on the arms and legs. Some wore extensive armor that covered the body, the length of their arms and their legs. They were armed with a broadsword and a shield but did not have the ability to move with speed and were reliant on their armor and their weapons for defense".

"Gladiators were divided into different categories dependent on their weapons and their fighting styles, for example some preferred to fight with short swords and others with long swords. There was also the standard issue military sword but in reality the dimensions of a gladiator's sword was solely reliant on the gladiator. Most master swordsmen have their swords forged to suit their needs".

She continued to explain. "In the beginning we all started with wooden swords and wooden shields, fighting with our trainers and tutors. Once we were adept at it, we were allowed metal swords, armors and shields and our first real opponents were guard dogs from the mines, who were rabid infested and mad. Despite being armed and armored they were by no means easy victims and it took me at least three tries to learn to anticipate the savagery of a rabid dog".

"I realized that it is possible to anticipate the moves of a rational opponent but impossible to predict the movement of an irrational opponent. Part of winning is anticipating." Usan and Nawang nodded their heads in agreement. It was essential in any dual to be able to predict your opponent's actions.

"Then we moved on to friendly opponents before being elevated to the status of fighting real opponents. It was a crucial battle for everyone concerned because captives who were victorious were granted their freedom and therefore they fought with unmitigated savagery. It was an actual fight to the death and crowds thronged in the thousands to witness the colossal battles. The gladiator had to kill his opponent. Surrender was never an option for captives or gladiators. There was always the alternative of working in the slave mines for twelve years and becoming a part of Tarchem's great mining colony but some chose to fight their way to freedom in the arena which was of course futile given the caliber of gladiators that Tarchem churned out. But there were some who were braver than others and who chose death as opposed to serfdom".

"The final test of courage was to fight a wild animal, a lion, a tiger or a panther but often even a hyena or a jackal proved deadly. These fights also attracted big crowds and the outcome could go either way. Something about watching a person being torn to shreds appealed to the exuberant spectators".

"After becoming a gladiator of some note, I was promoted to the ranks of assassin. There is a big difference between an assassin and a swordswoman. The assassin had a wider means of bringing about the death of an enemy with the addition of subtle variations. I was placed under the tutelage of a grandmaster and under her guidance I learnt to kill not only with swords but with blades, daggers, ropes, clubs, poisons, blunt instruments and even my bare hands. Each method of killing required a special skill and mastery of it was not easy" she summed up.

It was the first time Usan and Nawang had heard her talk and it was refreshing to hear her voice. She was a pleasant speaker and eloquent when there was a need to be. They continued with their meal and Usan decided to extend their stay at the inn.

Usan was determined to set up a trading post in Zanskar. Most of the dwellings were rudimentarily constructed from wood and the carpentry left a lot to be desired. Many of the workers in the construction sector were part timers. They were hunters, wood gatherers and sometimes miners, who doubled up as builders because of climatic restrictions and weather conditions. They took to building work when seasonal changes hampered their normal work.

Hence there were very few specialists around. The town however had lots of potential. This could easily be ascertained from the volume of trade and the bulk of goods that changed hands. The townsfolk were not dressed in the bright colored clothes of Leh but were more content to dress in the informal tunics of workmen and laborers.

Even the merchants and tradesmen that frequented Zanskar dressed moderately to blend in with the rest of the crowd. Frontier towns in addition to attracting honest folks were also a destination for robbers, bandits and a host of other unsavory types that left a lot to be desired.

The market place was big as was to be expected and adequately furnished with huge stalls arranged in rows for retailers and merchants to peddle their wares. There were small warehouses constructed in the center of town, a strange place to position them but the town planners decided it was where the warehouses would be least prone to attacks and Zanskar being a trading town, was an obvious target.

The town was not designed to attract tourists and the odd sightseer was often bored by the lack of imagination or creativity that went into the construction of the buildings. Zanskar wasn't built to be artistically pleasing; it was built for practical functionality.

The town attracted a lot of rough types and towards the extreme end of the town there were bars, brothels and adult establishments that were designed to suit the needs of those with a more adventurous flair. These men were important to the town's economy and it only made sense to ensure that their needs were adequately catered for.

The town had a local constabulary that was commissioned by the town council with grudging approval from the king. The nobility disapproved of the formation of any militia apart from the standing army but made an exception in the case of Zanskar given its rather precarious location.

Zanskar was bordered by the Kush Mountains to the north and beyond that were the remains of the former Empire that had splintered into separate kingdoms. Rowina was the next kingdom and it was connected to Zanskar via mountain passes, routes that circumvented the mountain range or went over ridges and many of these routes were hidden in seclusion unknown even to the authorities.

These were some of the most dangerous routes in existence, used to ferry goods, commodities, arms and other supplies to meet the demands of profiteers and black marketers. It had been used by the rebels in Southern Rowina to acquire or procure the items that they needed for their war in the past.

Usan decided that it was worth establishing a link with some of the insurgent units or aspirant leaders in Rowina to further the aims and ambitions of Hawk's Nest. Amesha Spenta would undoubtedly be pleased with such a noteworthy arrangement and there was no harm in forging mutually beneficial ties with both sides in the conflict.

The trio scoured the marketplace taking closer order of proceedings, keeping their eyes peeled, looking out for possible stalls for rent or hire. There was plenty of space available that were much bigger and more spacious than the stalls that they used in Leh. The local authorities had evidently taken great care in putting together larger outlets more suited to the needs of the town.

They selected the stalls, this time closer to the entrance and went in search of the official in charge of the market place. They found him in an office that resembled a well-built shed. Usan knocked on the door and a young official no older than twenty five, bearing the bars of a captain on his shoulders answered. He was polite, clean shaven and he obviously took great pride in both his job and his appearance.

His name was Dawa. He was a medium built man, stocky and muscular, his skin slightly paler that the norm, which indicated that he came from the tribes of the north. He was prim and proper, and very attentive in his job. The matter was resolved within minutes with no additional charges or bribes. Usan paid the rent for a year and any other taxes, levies or charges that might be imposed. He liked the man and invited him for dinner at the inn.

Dawa even inquired if Usan needed any help procuring the supplies that he needed for his new stall. He had a list of vendors who were willing to work with newcomers. "I'll look into it" said Usan with a polite smile. They rented in total three stalls that they hoped to stock with various goods.

Unlike Leh where they had to ferry the goods from the point of origin to the marketplace, the situation in Zanskar was the reverse. Suppliers visited the stalls regularly with their merchandise, especially fresh produce, and all stall owners needed to do was to stack their stalls with the products that were brought in.

Usan made up his mind to not only stack the stalls in Zanskar but to also ferry the products to the stalls in Leh that were in reality retail outlets for the goods that they sourced. Kalden would be appointed to run the stall in Leh and Usan assigned himself the task of roving around creating more stalls. It was slightly disappointing because he wouldn't be able to see much of Dechen but if he intended to rise to greater heights, he had to make the necessary sacrifices.

The next couple of weeks flew by at the rate of knots and the trio busied themselves with stocking the stores with more supplies. They needed an extra pairs of hands and local laborers were employed to lift the goods from the shelves and stack them accordingly. Dechen's expertise in the field would come in handy and he thought it only prudent to send a note through Nawang to invite the young lady to give him a hand at her convenience.

If things panned out, it would give him a chance to spend some quality time with Dechen and Nima which he was sure would be appreciated all around. Nawang was sent out almost immediately with almost little or no preparation. The scout was used to moving around at the slightest notice and his days in the army had taught him to be always alert and be prepared to travel at short notice.

As a boy he had grown up with hunters who had taught him most of his scouting and tracking skills. He would wait for hours hidden in the bushes with his father, as still as a church mouse watching and listening for signs of his quarry. Deer was the preferred animal; venison meat was much sort after, both for consumption and for retail.

The Betan Plateau didn't prohibit deer hunting but it was limited to certain seasons to stop the sudden depletion of deer stocks. He had to learn to follow animals through their tracks, signs and trails. Animals, like mortals, always left behind telltale signs like imprints, scents and droppings.

He had to learn how to remain downwind because some animals especially deer had a keen sense of smell and if they even got as much as the whiff of a man they would scatter and flee.

As he got closer to his quarry, he had to make sure that the animal was firmly in his sights without it catching as much as a glimpse of him. Deer sometimes kept looking back down the trail, remaining on the lookout out for any danger that might be lurking around.

Animals exuded spoors. When the spoor is fresh, it meant that the animal was close. Trackers had to wait patiently or else the animal might spot them coming. A fresh spoor usually meant that that their quarry was close.

Deer usually rested facing downwind, so that it could see danger approaching from the blind side and may also double back on its spoor and circle downwind before settling down to rest.

Trackers had to move with stealth and walking in the bushes was very different to walking along the cobble stoned pavements of Leh. Hunters placed the balls of their feet on the ground first and then slowly brought down the rest of the feet feeling for any twigs and dry branches on the ground that might give away their presence.

Kills were best made from a distance, with a bow and an arrow. Nawang was introduced to the bow early in his life and over the years he had mastered the skill to kill from a distance. The sword came in much later and it was used more for self-defense than as a mode of attack. As a young lad he had to step in and out of rough frontier towns and he needed to know how to use a blade in order to get himself out of awkward situations.

The skills that he learnt came in handy when he joined the Royal Betanese Army where he was deployed as a scout. He excelled in the role and had no fear of being the first in line. He knew that if he made a mistake it was his head that would be the first to roll but that didn't faze him or intimidate him in the least bit.

While Nawang was away, Usan delegated the task of overseeing shipments to Nima. She proved to be a better organizer than he expected and he marshaled the whole affair with a smile on his face.

Usan decided that his stalls would sell garments, fresh produce, pottery and much sought after silverware including little trinkets. He scouted around for a stall that sold good food and had food delivered to his new stalls for breakfast, lunch and dinner so that his workers never went hungry.

After her unexpected "opening up" Nima seemed more receptive to conversation and didn't appear to be adverse to any relevant hints or suggestions that Usan dropped. The girl was an able lieutenant but he doubted that his short stint at the top would last for long. He was certain that Karmina would assume the role in due time, with or without his consent.

He wasn't wrong. His sister appeared like clockwork within a fortnight and went to work on the new stalls. Dechen had graciously agreed to help leaving her own stall in the hands of able assistants.

Usan was happy to see Dechen again and he walked up to her and gave her a gentle peck on the cheek ignoring even his sister. Karmina stood silently by and watched as her brother strolled up to the young lady, leaned over and kissed her on the cheek.

Karmina let the moment pass uninterrupted before assuming control. She had the girls working in tandem while the men were relegated to more menial tasks. Usan however, given his infinitely superior position as master spy was spared. Within a week of her arrival he was on the road again with Nawang and Nima scouring the plateau for more stalls.

In the following months the trio had managed to establish stalls and outlets in almost every major town in the Betan Plateau and Usan was fast making a name for himself as head of Usan Holdings, a trading house of good repute.

The Usan Holdings headquarters was set up in the plateau's capital, Gilgit. The town was more contemporary in appearance but its occupants were more conservative. It was also the Headquarters of the Betan Chamber of Commerce and Usan with the help of Dechen whose father was coincidentally the President of the Betan Chamber of Commerce was formally admitted into the organization.

He was given a minor position with the promise that he would soon be elevated up the ladder depending on his performance. Dechen of course had a major hand in the whole affair and she managed to convince her father to give the young man a chance.

In the meantime Sonum had returned from the Alchemic Sisterhood, and was in Leh assisting Kalden with the stall there. It was a precarious time for both institutions given the dire predicament most of the kingdoms were in, as the Dark Lord's emissaries continued to infiltrate and transgress their borders.

The process of gathering and processing information was also attended to in earnest and both Karmina and Usan busied themselves with sifting through the information that they had received, separating fact from fiction.

Thus far no one knew the identity of the Dark Lord for certain but it was widely accepted that he was a disciple of the abyss. According to intelligence reports there was a temple that was located in the heart of the Central Kingdoms and many years ago a child was found on the doorstep of this temple.

The temple was dedicated to Ahriman or Angra Mainyu, the very epitome of evil. According to legend after he descended from the sky, he resided among men for eons. Eventually he tired of the mortal race and retired to eternal slumber in a marble temple that had as its altar a sacred crypt. It was assumed that beneath the crypt of polished black marble was the living chamber of Ahriman. In reality however the crypt was a portal to a world of lavish pleasures that Ahriman had created for himself.

The king and queen were childless for years, but were faithful supplicants of Ahriman. After a decade of service to him a child was bequeathed to the King and Queen as a reward for their unwavering loyalty. In time the child assumed the mantle of leadership and became known as the Dark Lord. Some reports suggested that he was the son of Ahriman himself but the name of his mother remained unknown.

Ahriman had great power and he shielded the Dark Lord. It was a well-known fact that he exercised some influence over the Guardian of the Abyss but exactly how much influence was yet to be determined. The intelligence committee in Hawk's Nest was under the impression that

Ahriman and the Dark Lord planned to open the gates of the abyss and unleash the demons that were locked away behind its infernal gates. It would not be the first time in history that it had happened and the last opening of the gates had led to the collapse and eventual demise of the Grand Empire.

From records derived from the time he roamed the earth among men, Ahriman is described as a bronze Adonis of superior strength and intellect, towering well above the rest, gifted with the skill of persuasion and magic beyond mortal comprehension. He was a being without equals and among men he was unchallenged and unparalleled.

Usan V

"*They may promise that a place will be awarded in the kingdom of heaven or the afterlife to any warrior who helps overthrown an enemy king. They may promise an eternity of bliss to any upstart who helps dispose or neutralize an enemy*"

"*Spies are allowed to venture into agriculture, cattle rearing and other forms of subsistence in the lands and chattels allotted to them. They are also allowed to acquire new lands and chattels for that purpose. These spies are allowed to become merchants and traders and are allowed to build and expand their enterprise*"

"*From the profits thus acquired, the chief spy or master spy is required to provide all his subordinates with suitable remuneration, clothing and lodging, and send them on espionage missions, ordering each of them to detect a particular kind of crime committed against the religious order and to report it when they returned to receive their wages*"- Hawk's Nest

❖❖❖

The pair forwarded their reports to Amesha Spenta and the overlord. They encouraged their small but growing number of workers that presently numbered just over thirty to speak to their customers and to gather as much information as possible, commercial or military especially with regards to the activities and whereabouts of the Dark Lord.

Karmina also sent a note to the First Minister of Rowina to request for his approval to open a new trading outpost in the kingdom. The plan was simple, to forge an alliance with both the governing monarchial institutions and with the rebels of Southern Rowina. They needed allies on all fronts.

The kingdom itself was best described as a conglomeration or consortium of agricultural tribes that had transformed to become a lethal fighting force during the Dark Ages, a period when chaos reigned and the house of death had many frequent visitors. It was a triumphant time for the queen of the abyss and according to myth she had ventured forth from her palace of infamy in the darkest region of the underworld, to set foot on the earth for the first time. Ereskigal, the queen of the netherworld neither feared nor heeded the rays of Shamash. For like him she too was a god and a god of infinite power at that.

Good knowledge of the land and its people formed the basis of stoic alliances. Usan and Karmina studied as much as they could about the Kingdom of Rowina before they forwarded their proposal. Usan led the team with Karmina, Dechen, Nima, Nawang, Dorjee and Sonum. The priestess from the Alchemic Sisterhood had insisted on being present. The journey to Rowina was perilous and despite having fashioned an alliance of sorts with the rebels, other feuding lords and bandits still roamed freely and were a force to contend with.

The road was winding and the journey was slow. They often had to watch out for falling rocks that rolled down from the summit of the mountain. Usan rode in the lead with Nawang. He was in a personal dilemma and had eventually realized the futility of flirting with three women. The present situation was embarrassing to say the least worsened by the fact that the women were all on good terms with his sister and they all got along famously well together, to the extent that they sometimes ignored him. Usan had abandoned the idea of a harem and decided to return to the most glorious institution of priesthood where he started and devote his spare time to worshipping the gods.

That night after pitching the tents, while the ladies busied themselves with preparing a meal of Yak's meat mixed and blended with herds and wild mushrooms, Usan excused himself and spent hours chanting mantras that he had ignored in the months that he had been away from Hawk's Nest.

He found an inner peace within himself and remembered his time at the monastery as a young boy, when on a calm and still morning he had caught the scent of blood and carnage in the air. He knew then that they were embroiled in a bitter war and his sister was right. They had no time to be frivolous or flippant given the dire situation in the other kingdoms.

Hawk's Nest had mobilized the order of the Emerald Knights, the fourth highest order in Hawk's Nest headed by the leader of a lesser sect to engage in open campaigns against the knights of darkness. From all accounts the fate of Lamunia hung in a balance and it was impossible to predict or forecast an outcome.

The opposing sides were caught in deadlock in the center of the kingdom and neither side appeared to be giving in an inch. Lamunia had been reduced to a battle ground with both forces firmly and deeply entrenched. The Emerald Knights recruited carpenters from the south to not only build their encampments but to also build catapults. Trees were felled and siege engines that were used to batter the formidable walls of castles were used instead to pelt the enemy with showers of stones that were covered in tar and set alight.

The result was devastating. Morbid screams and the nauseating smell of burnt flesh filled the air. The enemy however remained undeterred and the brutality of the attack did nothing to lessen their resolve. The Emerald Knights were led by a young princess called Natasha. She was no older than twenty five with hair as blonde as the radiant sun. Natasha was of noble blood and excelled in both war and worship. At birth she was gifted with the armor of the sun which bestowed upon her the gift of invincibility. She could only be defeated if she gave her armor away.

The inhabitants of Rowina dressed differently to the people of the Betan Plateau and according to intelligence reports the weather in Rowina was unpredictable and was mild at best, with the exception of the southernmost province where climatic conditions were similar to Betan. In the north of the kingdom unexpected changes in the weather could send the temperatures plummeting.

The inhabitants had their swords strapped to their sides and were clad not only in fur boots but in armor forged from molten metal. Mail shirts were the norm and they were fairer and taller than the inhabitants of the plateau.

Karmina assumed the mantle of leadership, a foregone conclusion that was long decided, despite Usan's authority as master spy. She had managed through the aid of her emissaries to secure a suitable location for their new venture. Unlike merchants in the plateau, merchants in Rowina did not operate on the stall concept. For starters the cold climate did not permit or make working in the open feasible.

Even at the height of summer temperatures sometimes remained low. The cold winds from the glacier filled peaks of the Kush Mountains blew down on the kingdom bringing with it ice, sleet and snow. Wooden fires were needed to keep the stores warm.

Karmina had managed to purchase a store in the largest town in Central Rowina, Dacia, with the help of both the nobles and the rebels. A disgruntled owner who had been a thorn on the side of the rebels by publicly denouncing them and had siphoned away some of the levies belonging to the crown was suddenly found mysteriously dead, in a dark alley, lying in a pool of blood.

The council had forfeited his store for refusing to pay the taxes, and auctioned it to claim the outstanding levies. Karmina was given first preference when his possessions were put up for sale. It was a discreet arrangement that no else knew anything about.

She purchased the store complete with furnishings and stock and with the help of Dechen she hoped to transform the store into a profitable enterprise to finance further ventures in Rowina. So far everything was going according to plan but she was not averse to the fact that Rowina presented a new set of challenges and her team had to attune themselves to their new surroundings.

The journey across the Kush Mountains took approximately a fortnight and it was largely uneventful. Their biggest obstacles did not come from bandits but marauding wolves that scoured the hillside searching and foraging for meals.

Unlike the wolves of the south these wolves were much bigger and much heftier. They travelled in packs like most wolves but were many times more daring than their southern counterparts chancing their luck even against armed riders.

It became a bit of challenge to keep the wolves away from the horses and company had to stand guard nightly in the light of blazing fires, armed with bows and arrows, to prevent the horses from being reduced to wolf feed.

The arrows even with the added advantage of being fired from a crossbow did little to reduce the severity of the attacks. Nima proved up to the challenge when she fought off a wolf single handedly. After a prolonged battle she managed to severe the head from the body of the offending animal with a single swift stroke. The victory reminded her of her days in the Tarchem arenas and it brought a glow to her face.

Usan made a mental note to never get on the wrong side of Nima. Something in the way she decapitated the wolf told him of her abilities. She had an admirable quality about her that would be cherished among the ranks of the warrior priests.

Despite the attacks they managed to reach Dacia unscathed. The difference was striking and it was as if they had stepped into a whole new world. The design of the structures was in total contrast to what they were used to. Rowinian dwellings had triangular shaped roofs, as opposed to the flat roofs of the Betan Plateau and the walls were tiled with red bricks. There was a lot glass that was used in the construction process that displayed a spectrum of colors and an array of designs. The locals called it stained glass and it was peculiar to the north.

The town and villages that they had passed thus far looked much calmer than the towns in Betan, devoid of the crowds that normally thronged the streets of towns like Leh and Gilgit. As they rode down the main street, they noticed that most of the doors were closed, probably to keep the cold out and the buildings were insulated with wood and other materials. The stores resembled large cottages

No one seemed to take much notice of them as they entered the town precinct. With the exception of the odd turn of the head or the nudge of acknowledgement which obviously served as a greeting, they didn't say much.

The locals had rugged features, sculpted by the weather and molded by the environment. Little fires could be seen burning in tiny hearths and folks huddled around trying to keep warm. Usan couldn't wait to get indoors. After a fortnight in the cold, he missed the warmth of the southern sun.

The store that Karmina had purchased was a two storey building and the previous occupant had used the upper floor as his residence. Karmina modified the upper floor and turned it into a dormitory with separate sleeping quarters for men and women. The living quarters looked to be a modest but comfortable setup equipped with a kitchen and other amenities.

To some extent and if one didn't take into account the perilous journey across the Kush Mountains, the place could be classed as a holiday retreat. They tumbled in, sorting themselves out as they did, trying to get out of the cold as quickly as possible, after leaving their horses at a stable close by.

They headed straight for bed and in the days that followed they spent their time organizing the store. Instead of fresh produce they decided to carry clothes including male and female accessories especially those made from fur and leather. The previous owner despite his unpopularity had managed to establish a reasonably lucrative business and they scouted around for able staff to help man the stores when they were away.

Within a few days of their arrival members of the local council paid them a visit and Usan made sure that they were suitably entertained and that their needs were attended to, including the hefty levies that needed to be paid. Similarly a member of the largest rebel outfit also paid them a visit albeit in a more non-imposing manner. Usan and the others were invited to a cordial meeting, in the presence of Jedzimir, the most feared warlord in Rowina.

He controlled and area called the Southern Corridor and it included all the routes between the southern half of the former empire and the northern half of the former empire, and the routes along the Kush Mountains.

Nothing passed through the man-made cordon without either implied or express consent from Jedzimir. He was the most controversial figure in the region and his popularity swung from one extreme to the other.

As a young lad, Jedzimir was schooled at home. His parents were poor serfs who could not afford a formal education. He showed great aptitude and was soon ahead of his peers. He excelled in both studies and sports and was well versed with all the religious texts. No one had been able to get close enough to him as yet to determine if he was gifted with the talent.

Thus far he had managed to evade all attempts on his life and elude any trap that had been set for him. His lieutenants were just as elusive as he was. Jedzimir was a man that, according to all accounts, had a private army at his disposal.

Blacksmiths, ironmongers and other industries related to the supply and the manufacture of arms blossomed like wild mushrooms in the area around the Southern Corridor to furnish the needs of the rebels, financed by the rebels themselves. The rebels operated openly in the Southern Province and its inhabitants maintained a veil of secrecy.

So it came as a bit of a surprise when an invitation was extended to Usan. It may have had something to do with the fact that Karmina had secretly arranged for medical supplies and other basic amenities to be ferried to them. She also provided them with food and other provisions at almost no or reduced costs. It was in the interest of Hawk's Nest to ensure that neither the nobles nor the rebels grew more powerful than the other and therefore they created a mechanism whereby they could balance the interest of the nobles with the serfs.

The journey to the rendezvous point began after just sunrise following morning prayers and despite being away for more than a year the pair remained faithful in worship. Usan admittedly had been a bit wayward in recent times but was once again showing signs of progress.

Without realizing it, he was becoming the master spy that he trained so hard to be. With his sister's help he had developed an extensive network and was on the verge of elevating himself to a diplomatic career within the ranks of the Betan Chamber of Commerce.

The journey took them through a warm and sometimes desolate land and during the long but informative journey they managed to witness some of the rites and rituals of the locals. The natives here had a peculiar burial rite. The body of the deceased was left on an elevated platform in a lonely secluded area for vultures to feed on.

The occupants of the south adhered faithfully to many of their ancient covenants. Among these, was their custom of the disposal of the dead, which, however peculiar it may appear to others, was by far a natural, appropriate and acceptable method of sanitation. It was nature's way of ensuring that life regenerates. Their burial rites were based on the notion of preserving all possible respect for the dead, before and after the separation of the soul from the body.

The body in accordance with stipulated customs should be disposed of in a way that is least harmful and least injurious to all living beings.

Usan reflected on the customs of these ancient people and realized that even in death there is life and the carcass that falls away continues to provided nourishment and sustenance for the earth and the living. Nature on its own was at perfect equilibrium.

As the hour of death approaches preparations are made for the disposal of the body. The compartment in the house, where the body is placed, is washed and cleaned with soap and water. The white shroud in which the body is to be wrapped in must also be washed even if it was newly purchased.

Priests are summoned to assemble round the death bed and recite prayers that will help the spirit repent for the sins it had committed. If the spirit realizes its fault or mistakes the transition to the next life is made all that much easier.

The priests are paid in money and corn for their attendance. It is beneficial to the spirit if the person just prior to death is able to join the priests in saying the last repentance prayer.

The spirit of the man who has recited the prayer of repentance towards the end of his life, a prayer praising good thoughts and good deeds and condemning bad thoughts and bad deeds is quicker to find salvation than the spirit of the man who has not.

It is said that one recital of the repentance prayer towards the end of one's life is worth the entire region of khvaniratha, which is the most propitious and most auspicious region among the seven regions of earth.

A short time before death, the dying person is made to drink a few drops of consecrated haoma water. Haoma is a plant that symbolizes immortality and a few drops of water added to its juice by priests after performing the haoma ceremony in any temple of the eternal fire, gently dropped into the mouth of the dying person, will guide the spirit upon death to the next life or the hereafter.

At the time of death a fire is lit fuelled by pieces of dried wood, butter and ghee. Priests sit before the flame and continue to recite sacred verses until such time as the body is to be removed to the tower of silence. It is enjoined that the priests and all persons should sit at a distance of at least three paces away from the dead body.

Following the sacred rite, the body is carried to the tower of silence. This can be done at any time during the day but it is essential that the body is exposed to the sun. It is strictly forbidden to carry or even move the body by night.

The body must be borne by at least two corpse bearers even if the deceased is an infant. No person should be allowed to carry the dead alone.

The number two plays a prominent part in all ceremonies relating to the dead. From the time the departed releases his last breath the body must never be left alone or attended to by a single person. The number two becomes significant from the time of death.

According to the ancient scriptures, the soul of a dead person remains within the precincts of the mortal world for three days. During this time the spirit witnesses its past deeds that replay before its eyes in quick successions. If the spirit belongs to someone who has led a pious life, it sees lovely images flash before it and it is filled with joy and happiness.

If the spirit is that of a wicked person, it sees images of demons and other vulgar beings. It shudders and trembles in unhappiness and is at a loss. In accordance with these images the spirit of the righteous man directs itself to paradise and the spirit of the unrighteous man directs itself to hell.

For the three days and nights that the spirit remains within the precincts of the mortal world, it is under the special protection of Srosh Yazad. Srosh is the guardian of all spirits of the dead. "O most radiant Srosh who shines with the effulgence of a thousand suns, protect our loved ones here and in world between death and rebirth, in the world that is neither material nor spiritual" - implore the relatives of the deceased.

If the surviving relatives cherish the memory of the departed and remember Srosh with gratefulness and if they try to please Srosh with pious thoughts, pious words and pious deeds, it is most likely that Srosh will take an interest in their welfare and assist them when required.

The same prayer is also recited at night before one falls asleep to invoke the protection of Srosh, who is but the guardian angel.

<hr />

The human body is divided into two components, the physical component which the locals call gaetha and the spiritual component which they refer to as mainyu. The mortal being is a combination of gaetha and mainyu. While the gaetha is limited to a certain time and space the mainyu is infinite and exists for the duration of time. The mainyu or the spiritual aspect of the body is divided into three components. Urvan, fravashi and pahlavi.

Urvan is the soul of the mortal body that continues to exist after the physical body falls away following the transition between death and rebirth. Some souls are pure and others are tainted but at the end all souls will be cleansed and will return to adjoin with the Brahmatma.

The second spiritual component is that which resides in all matter. This component is called the fravashi or the minute personification of the super soul that exists in all things.

The super soul is the collective consciousness that links all things, the created and the uncreated together and collectively all things created and uncreated make up the super soul. Fravashi means the place in which god resides or the fourth dimension and every bit of matter in existence contains a minute quantity or aspect of the fourth dimension.

The final component of the soul is called the pahlavi. The pahlavi is the archetype for all persons, an icon that all persons can emulate. It is embodied with the characteristics of the God of Gods, Ahura Mazda.

The righteous entity seeks to emulate all the positive qualities of Ahura Mazda. It is a brilliant, radiant, positive, constructive and beneficent being that constantly seeks wisdom.

Time for the Mazdanians is divided into two categories, mortal time that is measureable and quantifiable and immortal time that is immeasurable or unquantifiable. The latter is also referred to as time from the perspective of the super soul or the Brahmatma.

The goal in life is to achieve abiding spiritual resplendence, happiness, and peace. An individual who is at peace with himself is at peace with humanity itself. Spiritual resplendence confers on a person wisdom and enlightenment. It is a path that leads to a meaningful and fulfilling existence. The spiritual self is the beacon that lights the path ahead and once this beacon is realized all things will become clear.

Like those who are faithful to the teachings of Hawk's Nest turn to Safa the god of flames, the most resplendent messenger of the gods for guidance, the people of the Southern Province also turn to the flames for guidance. Their flame is called athra or the source of all physical and spiritual light. At the heart of all worship burns a flame that is continuous and everlasting symbolizing an eternity of serenity.

The flames represent the ethical values of asha: honesty, order, fairness and justice. It is the values behind the flame that must be understood.

Usan VI

"All public appearances by the chief spy or master spy will be coordinated by their subordinates and all public exhibitions will be preplanned to achieve the desired outcome and leave the audiences enthralled by the performance or exhibitions of the chief spy or master spy"

"It is the duty of the spy to gain access to all major institutions and discover the causes of quarrels, if any between them. These may include anger, jealousy and greed. It also is the duty of the spy to sow the seeds of well-planned discontent among enemy allies. Discontent is nurtured when the need arises and harmony is fostered when it is require. All things are done in accordance with the needs of the sect".

"In all disputes monies become relevant and the noble institution of spies must help its allies with financial assistance when it is require" - Hawk's Nest

---

The soil in the south was fertile and dead organic matter which decomposed into black humus gave the soil a dark shade which permeated through to the surface nourishing it with nutrients. An extensive network of canals made agriculture a viable option. Usan and the rest could only sit back and admire the ingenuity of the architects who had pioneered the astounding hydraulics project.

There was only one major river, the Sanges that flowed through the Kingdom of Rowina. It started at the snowcapped peaks of the Kush Mountains and dissected the country in half before eventually flowing into the icy cold waters of the Northern Sea.

The canals that were designed to bring waters to homes and farms within the city were constructed to the highest standards in order to satisfy the requirements of the province. The walls of these magnificent engineering feats were lavishly adorned with inscriptions.

The heat coupled with the swerving cool crisp water that came streaming down from the glacier filled summit of the Kush Mountains contributed to the humidity of the area. Unlike the fertile farmlands of the north that were planted with high yielding staple crops, the farms of south were laden with orchards filled with apricot, apple and olive bearing trees. Grapes were also a viable commercial option that local growers had embraced with a passion.

Grapes grew well in the humus rich soil and were used to make wine. Grapes from this region were much sort after by wine makers. It produced some of the best wines in the kingdom.

They didn't rush their journey; fully aware that Jedzimir had eyes everywhere in the south and would have been alerted to their presence as soon as they had crossed the invisible borders that acted as the great dividing range.

Sonum had taken a keen interest in the area, taking in as much as possible storing it in her memory. Members of the Sisterhood had an astonishing memory. They were endowed with the ability to create mental replicas of everything that they saw and they didn't have a need for written records. Over the years this detail had proved vital to their survival because enemies of the Sisterhood were unable to intercept any communiqué between them. Like those who belonged to Hawk's Nest they too believed in the concept of collective memory only theirs was more attuned.

The sisters shared the memory of Tiara, the founder and the first High Priestess of the Alchemic Sisterhood and all the sisters that followed. The common perception was that the memories of the High Priestess was linked directly to the fourth dimension but no one could say for certain because the Sisterhood operated in the strictest confidentiality.

In time the sisters had managed to harness their talents and had discovered a way to pass the knowledge that was stored away in the labyrinths of their minds to the next generation. In this aspect they had even surpassed the abilities of the warrior priests.

There was some correlation between the religious doctrines that permeated all four cultures and therefore they had common grounds to work off, expand and explore. These unifying principles were essential to secure the alliance between Hawk's Nest, the Sisterhood, Rowina and Jedzimir's men.

The discontent in the south did not stem from the diversity in religious perceptions. It was in reality the inequitable distribution of wealth that saw the peasants deprived of the rewards for their labor. Much of it had to do with greed. It was but a fallacy of human nature that had boiled over into a major conflict.

The noblest of people can be reduced to fragments and shred to pieces by constant toil and turmoil. War was essentially a conflict between two forces that had existed since the dawn of time and will continue to exist until the end precipitated by the subjective perception of good and evil.

Trade on the other hand was solely motivated by an exchange of goods and services for monies or monies worth and it was by far a more enticing proposition than being a warrior for Usan. Despite his fidelity and his loyalty towards his religion, Usan felt that his rightful place in society was as a trader or a merchant. No doubt he was a spy but that was of little relevance. Information was knowledge and the exchange of information was a viable commercial enterprise.

Knowledge especially the kind that he possessed was a valuable commodity and worth huge sums of money to the right people. That's why rebel leaders like Jedzimir sought to keep their whereabouts a secret. No doubt there would be those who might be tempted to dispose of him should the opportunity present itself.

He saw no evidence of suppression or oppression and the community that Usan witnessed was thriving. It was an inspiring journey and it gave him time to ponder and mature and turn his thoughts to something that was more enterprising. From all indication, the Southern Province housed a highly evolved culture and perhaps it was the lack of understanding of the founding principles of the community that gave rise to the inherent problems. All things are a matter of perception.

They made it to the rendezvous point without any great difficulties and in accordance with the stipulated time. It was a large barren field and from the message that he had received, Usan was instructed to set up camp and wait for Jedzimir's signal. Karmina took charge once again and Usan was content to sit back and let the lady take the lead.

They didn't bother posting any guards and Nawang for once looked relaxed. They all knew that they were being watched and it was pointless taking evasive measures especially when the watchers were friendly. "This place is nowhere close to being a sprawling metropolis but I feel that one could be content living here" said Dorjee to Usan when he got the chance. Usan nodded his head. He couldn't agree more.

There was a natural serenity to the region without the frills or spills of towns like Leh and Gilgit. Most of the people here were farmers or in occupations that were in some way related to the land. It was a tight knit community which was preoccupied with satisfying its own needs.

There were no elected officials or council members to enact or enforce laws. Religious doctrine formed the core of the legal system and when the covenants were broken or disobeyed, Jedzimir and his men stepped in to mete out punishment.

Soldiers rarely set foot in the south. In addition to the truce, there was an informal agreement in place. The nobility and elected officials did not interfere with the governance in the South and in return shipments, taxes and other levies were not interrupted or interfered with.

They camped there for three days without any sign of Jedzimir or his men. On the fourth day close to the stroke of midnight, they were woken up by the soft sound of hoofs treading gently on the sandy loam that they were camped on. Nawang was the first to spot the intruders followed by Nima who instinctively reached for the handle of her sword.

The moon was full and the silhouettes of men on horses were clearly visible. Usan made out four men in total. The horses were tall and stood at least seventeen hands in height which was indicative of war horses. He could also make out light armor on the horses which told him that their visitors were battle ready.

The company gathered in a group as they watched the men ride in. Dorjee added some wood to the fire to keep it going, while Nawang put a kettle on. It was going to be a long night and fresh coffee would not go amiss. Usan felt that he should take the lead and greet the rebel leader. He tried to pick out Jedzimir. From all accounts he was a warrior of the highest caliber, lethal and as wily as a fox. Usan pictured him to be somewhat like Triloka, the renegade Lamunian general who had been elevated to the status of god because of his exploits.

Triloka was tall with broad shoulders that slimmed to the waist, with a tan that resembled a bronze god and looks to match. Jedzimir from all accounts was a similar type of man. The three men that walked in front, all appeared to meet the requirements. The two on the right and left looked a little more subdued than the man in the middle. That must be him thought Usan. He looked like a leader of men, tall, arrogant, beaming with confidence with an unmistakable air of command. As they walked into camp Usan rushed to meet him and left the women in the company of the fourth man, a hooded priest clad in brown tunics who lagged behind at the rear.

Usan walked up to him and held his hand out with an air of confidence. "I'm Usan" he said, his voice beaming with authority. The man smiled and took his hand in his. "I'm Jibran" he replied. The color on Usan's face instantly went down a shade and his shoulders hunched a mite. He knew he had made a classic mistake, a clinical error in judgment that could have cost him dearly at another time. His sister fortunately had been clever enough to spot the true Jedzimir. He was none other than the hooded priest.

Jibran laughed as did his companions. Usan smiled, he knew when he had been outwitted and was man enough to admit it. They gathered around the fire in good spirits and sat down. The man in the cloak kept his hood on.

Dorjee handed mugs of coffee around and one of the men unwrapped a large loaf of brown bread that he had stashed away beneath his cloak. He flushed out a dagger that was neatly tucked in his right boot and cut away large portions which he generously handed around.

Usan took a bite of the bread and he had to admit it was the most the delectable slice of bread he had ever tasted. The bread was made from brown wheat, and bits of fruits including cherries were included during the baking process. Before completion it was dipped in wild honey and it tasted scrumptious.

Usan could not resist asking for more and the man kindly accommodated. Usan had a sweet tooth and the bread proved too great a temptation for him to resist. He dipped it in his coffee and it tasted all the more delicious.

They continued to chat in a jovial manner and the man in the hooded cloak chipped in. His speech was clear but cautious. Jedzimir's looks did not live up to his reputation. He was tall and slender. His voice was soft and pleasant and he sounded more like a scholar than he did a warrior.

An hour into the conversation, he stood up to remove his cloak and beneath was a slim man, his features smooth and pale. If anything he looked pretty. His hair was soft and shiny, his skin faultless and his hands were tender as he held it out to shake Usan's hand.

He had a quiet unassuming air about him and he reminded Usan instantly of Nima. A natural born killer, gifted with knowledge and experience. His eyes were deep and piercing and they looked like they could see right through a man. There was something else about him; he looked devoid of false compassion. He either felt it or he didn't. In either case it didn't really matter because he was the highest authority in the South.

They continued talking until sun up, before he invited the others to one of his training camps that lay hidden in the rocky forests of the Kush Mountains. Karmina took up the offer instantly and soon they were on their way.

The company rode for almost an hour deep into the mountains. The sun was well up before they reached the secluded location that was hidden away in the bushes. From the outside there appeared to be nothing unusual but as they ventured closer they could make out faint images of men clad in leather armor with swords strapped to their backs. They looked like trained soldiers who staffed what was evidently a training camp for new recruits.

Usan VII

"*Women may seduce disciples and worshipers in neighboring kingdoms under the guise of a priestess and gain the loyalty of their male followers, inciting them to declare their king "unholy and unrighteous". In the same manner they may impose their charms on any kindred of a hostile king and temp them with gold to win their favor or shift their allegiance*"

"*Ascetic spies operating as priests or monks are granted the power to declare that the gods will be angered and that great misfortune may befall the land in the manner of disease and pestilence, if their instructions are not complied with. They may further declare that drought and famine will swarm the villages and wild fires will plague the fields and forests, and torrential rain will cause unrelenting floods if an unfriendly monarch continues to reign, instigating neighbors and tribesmen to depose or dispose of the unfriendly king or leader*"

"*When there is a major disagreement or a falling out with a kingdom, allies of Hawk's Nest should be removed from their respective premises and relocated to a safe haven, where they should be allowed, to stimulate discord and disunity. Operatives should be employed to stage protests and create a public outcry where appropriate or required*"

"Trivial matters should be exploited when necessary and allowed to mature and fester into full blown disputes, and armed conflicts"

"Spies, under the guise of astrologers and others, should bring to the notice of corporations the noble characteristics of any prince, leader or ruler who is favored by Hawk's Nest. The religious order in turn will send monies, men, arms, medical supplies, food and anything else that is required to garner the support of partisans" – Hawks Nest

---

The Southern Province was once ruled by Baron Daalir, the second cousin to the former king who maintained a strong vice like grip on the economy. He was eventually overthrown following an armed rebellion. Laborers, merchants, tradesmen and disgruntled farmers joined forces to become part of the rebel militia. The revolution itself was an event of great symbolic significance.

Peasant and serfs mobilized and organized themselves in response to harsh working conditions imposed on day workers in orchards owned by the Baron and in response to conflicts over land tenures. The newly formed rebel militia called itself the Serf Guard.

The Baron used force to crush the clamorous and vociferous dissent by the farmers labeling it incendiary and provocative thereby setting the stage for a peasant resistance that evolved into an armed conflict of mega proportions. The battles that ensued in the aftermath of a declaration of war cost countless lives but because the fighting was done in the mountains away from the areas that were farmed many of the orchards remained intact with little or no permanent damage.

In the years that followed the initial uprising, the Serf Guard grew from a small peasant army to its present unprecedented strength. This growth, in part, was facilitated by the profits the rebels had derived from the illegal sales of goods produced in the region and funding from sympathizers both domestic and foreign.

The rebel policies were based on a communal foundation in line with the principles of a more proportionate distribution of income derived from the sales of natural resources including proceeds from orchards that were the main source of income for laboring peasants.

The peasant income at the start of the revolution was less than ten percent of the total profits while the Baron absorbed almost ninety percent of the earnings. The initial clashes were violent and there was much bloodshed during the battles between communal forces and forces loyal to the Baron. The violent trend escalated in the following years and included assassinations and hits by specialized squads.

Nima was familiar with the duties of such squads or groups who operated independently and strayed away from mainstream sentiments. Their duties were pure and simply to make the hit when it was required and in her case, she was a hired sword who didn't ask any questions.

These hits and assassinations were not always done with discretion and some were orchestrated to instill fear and were sometimes carried out in public, in an open and transparent manner. The rebels even left behind notes for forces loyal to the Baron.

Other acts of blatant disobedience included beheading any member of the Baron's retinue that fell into rebel hands and having their heads impaled on a stake for public viewing, while the decapitated body was left to rot in the middle of a busy street. The peasantry revealed itself to be a more active force that the Baron had anticipated and the ruling monarchy was taken aback by the intensity of the attacks. Compelled by the ferocity of the fighting it agreed to broker an informal truce.

Finally realizing that the Baron was unable to win the war, the monarchy intervened and granted the Southern Region some measure of autonomy declaring it the Autonomous Province of Southern Rowina.

The camp was located at the foot of a large hill and there were as many as sixty four large hills scattered around the main hill. Each hill was composed of a mixture of ashes from the fire temple and soil. On each natural elevation there was a fire shine and its flames were kept lit all day.

Over time as the ashes slowly piled up the elevations increased in height. The locals, including the rebel soldiers were known as fire worshippers or worshippers of the sacred flame. They were loyal to Mainyu Athra.

A brick foundation was located near the bottom of the hills and the bricks were more or less similar in dimensions. The hills were not natural but a culmination of ash, soil and grime that had accumulated over the years. The shapes and structures of all the fire temples were identical.

The biggest shrine stood on top of the lone hill that was surrounded by the sixty four other hills and it rose sharply above the plain. One ascended the hill by a winding path with a series of natural stone steps. The main temple, which was also the headquarters of the Southern Division of the Serf Guard, was on the very crest of the hill; it was octagonal in shape and composed of large un-burnt bricks.

It was a domed structure with eight walls, one for each direction on the compass, each wall equipped with a door and a door frame. Brick and stucco columns framed the doorways and supported the roof, giving it a pillared effect.

There was a small monastery that was connected to the main temple. The exterior wall, was twelve feet in height, with a parapeted walk connecting the main temple to the monastery, made of rough cobble stones.

Many of the recruits looked young and unmarried and appeared native to the Southern Province. The average age didn't appear to be over twenty five.

The men enlisted for a variety of reasons, including ideological views, friendship and peer pressure, as well as the desire for excitement and adventure. Whatever their reasons or motives were once they signed up everything changed. They were indoctrinated into the cause and all else became trivial and at times immaterial or irrelevant.

They looked a content lot and many of them had thus far been spared the harsh realities of war. There was a tangible hint of peace in the air that had thus far endured.

RISE OF A MERCHANT

By
Kathiresan Ramachanderam

Prologue

By the tenth year of the reign of the God King Amesha Spenta, Usan and Karmina with the help of their friends had managed to establish a trading outfit equal to any other in the known world. Commissioned initially to set up an outpost to harvest information, the pair had managed to convert their espionage mission into a viable commercial option and with the small fortune that they had accumulated from the proceeds of sales they were able to finance their operations without further aid or assistance from Hawk's Nest.

The Memorandum and Articles of Association for Usan Holdings (hereafter called "the company"), a document that set out the rules and guidelines pertaining to the operations of the company read as follows:-

Without prejudice, the power vested in the company in accordance with the rules of god include the following:-

- To purchase or acquire by any means necessary chattels and property without regard to boundaries, ideologies, believes, customs, conventions and traditions.

- To acquire, protect, prolong and renew, regardless of jurisdiction, any trademarks, patents, copyrights, trade secrets, or other intellectual property rights, licenses, secret processes, designs, protections and concessions.

- To disclaim, alter, modify, use and to manufacture under license or grant licenses or privileges when or where appropriate and to expend money in experimenting upon, testing and improving, inventions or rights which the company may acquire or propose to acquire.

- To obtain in whole or in part any business, goodwill, the assets of any person, firm, or company carrying on or proposing to carry on any of the businesses which the company is authorized to carry on.

- As part of the consideration for such acquisitions to undertake all or any of the liabilities of such person, firm or company, or to acquire an interest in, amalgamate with, or enter into partnership with or into any profit sharing arrangement and co-operation with any such person, firm or company.

- To give or accept, by way of consideration for any acts done on behalf of the company, any shares, debentures, debenture stock or securities that may be agreed upon, and to hold and retain, or sell, mortgage and deal with any shares, debentures, debenture stock or securities so received.

- To improve, manage, construct, repair, develop, exchange, let on lease or otherwise, mortgage, charge, sell, dispose of, grant licenses, options, rights and privileges in respect of, or otherwise deal with all or any part of the property and rights of the company.

- To acquire by any means necessary any item that may be deemed commercially viable or has the potential of being converted to monies or monies worth.
- To lend or advance money, with or without security to any person, firm, company or kingdom in any way and through any means.
- To enter into any arrangement with any kingdom or authority (domestic or foreign) that may be deemed conducive to the attainment of the company's objectives and to obtain from any such kingdom or authority any charters, decrees, rights, privileges or concessions which the company may think desirable and to comply with any such charters, decrees, rights, privileges, and concessions.
- To employ, train and maintain a standing militia to protect the vested interests of the company.
- To enter into agreement with any organization, body, registered or unregistered, recognized or unrecognized, overt or covert in furtherance of the company's needs.
- To facilitate by any means possible the acquisition of information on any matter regardless if it is pertaining to the company or otherwise.
- To remunerate any person employed by the company or any person acting on behalf of the company in such manner that is deemed appropriate.
- To support and subscribe to any charitable organization which may be for the benefit of the company, its directors or its employees.

- To expedite the recognition and acceptance of the company as a separate legal entity in all known kingdoms or territories.

Usan holdings was spearheaded by Usan himself but the day to day affairs of the company were managed by Karmina with the assistance of Sonum, Nima and Dechen. The rest were allotted their respective duties as the quartet deemed appropriate.

The company had managed to set up outlets in every major town in the Betan Plateau and having acquired a firm foothold in Southern Rowina, backed by support from the Royal Rowinian Army and the Serf Guard, they had managed to secure lucrative contracts.

Despite the truce that subsisted, the proprietors of Usan Holdings realized that it was in their interest to ensure that tensions still continued. Usan Holdings were the major suppliers of arms and military equipment, for example swords, daggers, shields, maces, lances, bows, arrows and all other equipment needed for the defense of the realm. Their craftsmen were innovative and constantly strived to improvise on existing designs to keep rivals and enemy agents at bay. They also furnished medical supplies and food to both sides in the conflict. They had been awarded lucrative contracts which they needed to fulfill and repeated orders ensured the growth of the company and kept the money flowing in. Therefore it was only prudent, where possible, to keep the rivalry simmering, without precipitating any actual loss of life. The promise of peace was often more profitable than peace itself.

The company had also managed to acquisition plants and manufacturing facilities in the secluded regions of the Kush Mountains to cater for the needs of both armies. Many of these facilities were initially started by the Surf Guard to provision for the needs of their combatants but the present situation resulted in a decrease in demand for arms and many of the smaller manufactures especially blacksmiths and forgers were having a difficult time making ends meet.

Usan and Karmina had stepped in to ensure that the production facilities remained open by acquiring a major stake in most of the ailing facilities. They began expediting arms shipments to Lamunia where the need for arms and other military equipment was dire.

To facilitate these shipments Usan Holdings ventured into freighting and forwarding. Their subsidiary company Usan Transport, a freighting agency, was slowly gaining a reputation for being forwarders of some integrity. Their runners were well trained in the skills required to run a forwarding agency and they carried out their duties with the required proficiency. The extensive network that they had built simplified the process, and with the right officials in their pocket their shipments ran smoothly without any hiccups.

The odd rogue or bandit outfit still persisted in giving them trouble on odd occasions but the escorts who accompanied their shipments comprised of well-trained members of the militia who had no trouble putting the enemy down.

Because the existing demand far outstripped supply in the battle torn Kingdom of Lamunia, many of the weapons were no longer forged on anvils with the exception of those made on special requests. The practice was discontinued in favor of selective forging and blacksmithing. Weapons made on special requests normally fetched a higher price and were tailored to meet the specifications of the warrior by a blacksmith and ironmonger of some skill and experience. It was reserved for those who served Hawk's Nest. Usan Holdings was granted the privilege by Hawk's Nest of being the sole procurer for the Emerald Knights.

Under normal circumstances, swords, shields, and other armaments were produced using casting and molding techniques. Standard die casting methods included pouring molten metal into forgers that were specially built for the purpose. It enabled Usan Holdings to meet the surging demand and to continue reaping the rewards.

The company also made the decision to saturate the market with substandard products labeled with fictitious brands some bearing the coat of arms of the Dark Lord in the hope that they would make their way into the hands of soldiers or rivals who opposed Hawk's Nest. The practice was called flooding and in most instances it was a mechanism that was used to disrupt the domestic supply chain and cause prices to plummet but here it was used to unsettle the enemy.

The second most lucrative income generator for the company was the sale of food. It order to further the enterprise and to expedite shipments, Usan Holdings purchased farms in the

Betan Plateau and with the help of its contacts in the Betan Chamber of Commerce acquired large farmlands situated in the scenic outskirts of the plateau. It also bought up hundreds of acres of orchards in the Autonomous Province of Southern Rowina.

The company embarked on an ambitious project to cultivate food crops and in the process conserve valuable natural resources like soil and water, which was deemed essential to the long term survival of the company and the locality. The foothills of the Kush Mountains were planted with high yielding crops both in terms of quantity and quality. In addition to that the orchards also served to improve the environment by arresting soil erosion and noxious gas sequestration.

Part of the problem with shipping fresh fruits and raw produce was that they tended to spoil or rot at a fairly rapid rate and one of the biggest challenges was to keep consumables fresh for as long as possible.

Fruits packed in layers of fine sand and stored in wooden crates lasted longer than otherwise. Cheese, which had a universal appeal, especially salted cheese, was dipped in whisky to preserve its lifespan. Fruits lasted longer in colder climates than it did in the heat and therefore fruits lasted longer in Rowina than in the Betan Plateau.

In order to preserve the longevity of fresh fruits, the company decided to invest in food manufacturing facilities that bottled the food in glass beakers prior to distribution. The fruits were harvested and sent to factories where men and women were employed to clean and cut the fruits, removing the seeds from the flesh. The fruits were then bottled and preservatives were added to extent their shelf life.

The five most commonly used preservatives were salt, lemon juice, rosemary extracts, vinegar and sugar. Salt was used as a preservative not only for fruit but also for meat and fish. Salt helped dehydrate harmful organisms and kept the food fresh for longer periods.

The second preservative that they used was lemon juice. Lemon trees were cultivated in the orchards of Southern Rowina and the fruits were harvested and sent to food manufacturing facilities. The unfiltered heat in the region coupled with the moisture than lingered in the air was conducive to the growth of lemon trees. The fruits were harvested and extracted for their juice. Lemon juice drains the water content from fruits and prevents spoilage and rotting. Rosemary extracts were also used of prolong the life of fruits. Rosemary leaves are plucked and distilled and the residue is used as a food preservative.

Pickling however was the most common method and the preferred method for fruits that were sent to the Betan Plateau. Fruits were added to vinegar solutions which were obtained from the fermentation of sugar and water.

The least used preservative was sugar. Like lemon juice it drained the water content from the fruits and prevented rotting. Once the fruits were prepared and bottled they were labeled under various labels that were patented by Usan Holdings and shipped out.

Arms and food were Usan Holding's major income generators but as per the articles of association, the company traded in almost any commodity that was deemed commercially viable. Minerals and textiles were also other major sources of income. The company was given the nod by Hawk's Nest to trade and dabble in the black market. It was a lucrative side business that helped sustain their growing operations.

The company also exported meat but chose not to export livestock. Having weighed their options they found it more feasible to export meat that had been slaughtered, cut, salted and packed before it was sent out. It was much easier and infinitely less painstaking than driving herds of goats from one end to the other.

The whole trading operation was also a front to gather information and inevitably bits of news filtered through the various channels. The team was often preoccupied by separating fact from fiction and much of the information that filtered through was indiscernible especially with regards to the activities of ascetics, monks, priests, shamans and witches who operated in ways that were relatively unknown to most men and women.

Rise of a Merchant I

It was a warm night, at the height of summer, when Usan stepped out of the premises of the Betan Chamber of Commerce. He made his way towards the stable, walking discreetly, as he often did, in an unobtrusive manner, when he heard a faint click from the rear. He ducked instantly just in time to hear the sound of a dagger whizz past his head. He kept low and heard it strike a lump of wood. The sound triggered a discreet thud, a faint echo that broke the hush of an otherwise silent night.

Usan turned just in time to see a shadow clad in black disappear into the darkness of the night. He waited momentarily, his eyes flickering right and left watching for any giveaway signs that might betray any assassin that remained hidden in the darkness but he saw nothing to indicate that he was in imminent danger. He suspected that it was a single assassin and he didn't think too much of it. He took it as a sign of his rising popularity.

It the five years that had gone by Usan had matured considerably and he was no longer the young man who had visions of grandeur playing repeatedly in his head. The cold harsh realities of life had bitten into him and taken hold of him like an infectious disease without cure. He had come to the point where he longed for his quiet life back in the monastery but he knew it wasn't possible, not in the immediate future anyway. Maybe in another thirty years Hawk's Nest would allow him to retire to a small monastery in the middle of nowhere where he could spend the remaining years of his life in silent worship.

It was not the first attempt on his life and he was certain it won't be the last. His agents had been hard at work trying to locate the identity of the aggressor and the Dark Lord was the most likely suspect. Usan had been a thorn in his side since the formation of Usan Holdings and he had made it almost impossible for the emissaries of the Dark Lord to formalize any alliances in Rowina. Usan dealt with both the nobles and the Serf Guard. Jedzimir the supreme commander of the rebels was a close friend of his.

With events in Lamunia coming to a head it was essential that the agents of the Dark Lord cut off or at the very least disrupt the supply lines to the Emerald Knights for them to have any chance of a victory. It was widely believed and speculated that Usan was the brains behind Usan Holdings but the stalwart of the company was in reality none other than his sister Karmina.

Karmina's role in Hawk's Nest as far as Usan was concerned remained undefined and it was known only to the God King and the overlord. Usan was content to hand the reigns of leadership to his sister and remain a puppet whose strings were pulled by the women behind the curtains. That however did not exempt him from being the most likely target of assassinations.

He stood up and quietly strode towards the stable. He made his way to his horse, a fine looking chestnut mare with a white star on her forehead. He had put the older mare to retirement and she was now in an orchard spending her days beneath an apple tree, munching on the fruits that had fallen to the ground and lazing away in the sunshine. It was the least he could do for an animal that had served him so well.

He waited patiently and watched as the stable hand saddled the horse. The young boy obviously knew what he was doing and was confident enough to perform his duties diligently. He started by brushing the horse to remove the loose hair off its back. If the hair wasn't removed it got wet and caused the animal great distress.

He then lifted the underside of the saddle pad that he had placed on top of a pile of old weather beaten rugs and brushed the inside of the pad with his bare hands feeling for any sharp and hard objects that might be stuck in the fibers that might cause discomfort to the animal. Once he was certain that there were none he placed the pad on its back.

He then lifted the saddle, flipping the right stirrup and girth strap over the saddle to get them out of the way before taking the horse by the reins and handing her back to Usan. Usan smiled at the golden haired young boy and handed him a few coins before he placed his food on the stirrup and climbed on the mare's back.

As he made his way out of the stable he caught the faint twinkle of stars in front of him. The moon was out in full and if memory served him correctly, it was the night that shamans held their séances and released the spirits of the dead that they held in captivity. Not that it made much of a difference to him. At this stage he was more concerned with the living than he was with the dead.

Gilgit was a big town, much bigger than Leh but it was less boisterous and many of the patrons that frequented the town came from the upper middle class portion or section of the community. It had its fair share of tap rooms and dance halls but the crowds were more reserved and most of them were too busy with keeping up appearances and therefore dispersed at the slightest hint or sign of trouble. News travelled fast in Gilgit and a gentleman or a lady could not risk losing his or her reputation by being caught in an uncompromising situation.

Usan resisted the temptation to step into one of the tap rooms for a glass of red wine. He felt like he carried the weight of the world on his shoulders and right now all he wanted to do was to spend some time to himself. The need for solitude had prompted him to make the journey from Leh to Gilgit alone.

He made it back to his lodgings in time for supper. He had a plate of cold meat and washed it down with a glass of red wine before he made his way to his room.

The room was well furnished with a large wooden fireplace at one end but because it was relatively warm the fire remained unlit. The walls were covered with golden textured paper and the roof was tiled with intricate hand painted slabs. There was an oak writing table with a chair located next to the bed. An inconspicuous glass of water stood silently on the table with a tall glass resting in its shade. The furniture was obviously imported from Rowina or some other Kingdom to the north of the Betan Peninsula where oak was plentiful. Usan couldn't help but admire the carpenter's handiwork. The woodwork was neat and well crafted. The furniture was exquisitely designed.

He changed into his night clothes, which were nothing more than a pair of faded yellow robes and said his prayers facing the full moon that was visible through an open window before turning and slumping unceremoniously into bed. He slept fitfully that night. He had repeated visions of a woman clad in white silken gowns holding a bloodied dagger in her hand. Her hair was long and raven black. She had a purple streak in her hair just above her forehead. Her eyes sparkled like wild sapphires, and her arm was held upright, fresh blood dripping to the ground from the blade.

He woke up in the middle of the night and said a prayer before he sagged back to sleep only to have his dreams intruded again by the unknown lady. He felt a gentle breeze drift in from the north and he was certain it touched his skin. He heard voices, soft melodic voices repeating a rhythmic line in harmonious fashion. It was captivating at first like a little tune and he felt himself falling deeper and deeper into an abyss when he suddenly found himself standing on the banks of a river.

Standing across him was a man, clad in black, and as soon as he saw him, his consciousness returned. He grew angry at the sight of the man and began yelling and swearing profusely. He felt hate, pure unmitigated, unadulterated hate, unlike anything he had ever felt before. Ahriman!! The word flashed into his head. The child of darkness walked once again in the world of the living.

He woke up drained and sapped. He could feel the wet sheets beneath him. He had been sweating profusely and his throat felt dry. He needed a drink of water and reached for the jug that stood on the table beside his bed and poured himself a glass. Its crispness relieved the thirst but he was too exhausted to move. He put the jug and the glass back and drifted once again to sleep.

He was woken up the next morning by the touch of golden rays that came streaming through the open window. The evil that had coerced him the night before had disappeared but its touch remained in his memory. He felt tainted; the unexpected intrusion had scarred him. He got up and dressed before he went downstairs for breakfast. There were very few patrons that frequented the inn in the early hours of the morning. He had the choice of tables and he picked one next to a large window. He felt like he needed to see life for all its worth.

He ordered a bowl of chicken broth and a pot of hot coffee. It arrived it quick time and he scooped mouthfuls of broth, scoffing it down with a wooden spoon. He looked up to see the crowd on the street gradually increase as the day got brighter. Despite the unexpected encounter the previous night, Usan enjoyed the time to himself. In the five years that had passed he had become more reclusive and he realized that as one reached the pinnacle more time was spent thinking than doing. It was perhaps the natural order of evolution.

He checked out after breakfast. Usan had come solely to Gilgit for the meeting at the Betan Chamber of Commerce and following what had been a formal but rather unfruitful gathering between the delegates from the various provinces, Usan decided to take his leave. He was one of the two Vice Presidents of the Betan Chamber of Commerce and his appointment had come fairly quickly partly due to the unprecedented growth of Usan Holdings and partly due to help from Dechen.

The journey from Gilgit to Leh lasted almost a week and it took him through several small towns and villages. He had arranged to meet Nawang in a town called Dhingri that was famous for its textile industry. The traditional dress of the people of Dhingri was unique. Their clothes were often hand embroidered and patterned with intricate designs. The dresses of the women normally consisted of long flowing gowns reaching down to the knees. Most of the women used a headdress and covered their necks with scarves. Dhingri produced some of the best scarves in the known world in terms of both design and quality.

Usan also intended to meet some of his regular suppliers. He did so ever so often to keep the rapport going and to ensure that their families were well. He took an interest in people. Initially it was women more so than men but in recent times the focus had shifted and his interest in women had waned considerably.

———◆◆✕◆◆———

Thousands of miles away, sitting in a dark room lit by hundreds of candles, devoid of either comfort or luxury, a group of twelve acolytes gathered around a black circle, with the picture of a hexagram painted in the middle, illustrated in white ink with symbols and characters printed on it in a random and disorderly manner. They characters were unusual and uncommon written in a language not of the known world.

As the hour approached sundown and as the pale orange of dusk lit the twilight sky, between the time the sun departed the sky and the land ushered in the moon, the acolytes started chanting in an alien, outlandish tongue before one of the them, the chief preceptor who presided over the ceremony reached for a golden goblet filled with a thick red liquid. He lifted the chalice to his mouth and took a sip of the dense liquid before passing it on to the next priest on his left who after taking a sip passed it on to the next. The goblet made its way around the circle before finally returning to the chief preceptor.

He lifted the chalice with both his hands pointing to the sky and his head looked to the heavens. He murmured in a rhythmic manner and spilled what remained in the goblet onto to the center of the dark circle. The red liquid landed in a large blot forming a tiny pool on the surface of the circle. A closer inspection would reveal that it was not wine as many would have suspected but blood and if one were to hazard a guess it was not the blood of an animal but that of a maiden. Blood was the paramount elixir, of extreme and supreme importance in demonic rituals and the blood required for summoning differed from that which was required for appeasing. The blood for the former was that of a maiden, pure, undefiled, untarnished and untainted, born at a specific time, on a certain day of a specific month. Precise calculations were required to summon and convoke demons higher up in the hierarchy. The stronger the demon that was intended to be summoned the more complex the arithmetic that was required.

The priests continued their incessant chanting. It was repeated in a constant and perpetual manner until the blood in the center of the circle began to glow. Twilight had departed and night descended upon the earth. The blot of blood, transformed itself into a ring of unwholesome fire, without smog nor odor, without fume nor smoke, its radius widening outwards increasing in size at a rate of knots consuming everything in its path before finally materializing into a man, whose skin emitted an unsettling golden hue. The acolytes fell to one knee, heads held down and arms outstretched before they prostrated on the ground to welcome the new arrival.

Within the walls of the Temple of Druj the underlings gathered for the final kill. The High Priestess smiled, Ahriman would be pleased and the killing of the mortals would deepen the enmity between the age old rivals. Hawk's Nest would not be happy with the deaths of their favorites. They thought too highly of themselves, all too eager to destroy any creature from the dark realm. Hawk's Nest treated them with disdain and contempt, never wanting to comprise and were overly eager to reach for their swords. Amesha Spenta was the worst and the most feared because he was as vengeful as wrath. She wondered if she should send a message through her emissaries, to Aeshma, the fiend with the wounding spear, but soon decided against it. She was unpredictable and was best left to her own devices.

The underlings gathered around in a circle sitting in front of a table equipped with a large mirror. Outside the sun was fading as the solar barge sailed into the harbor. The forest was once again shrouded in darkness. Nothing here moved after sunset. It was no longer the hour of the living; it was the hour of the dead. As darkness inched closer, clouds began to fill the skies, blocking any light from seeping through and demonic spirits emerged from their subterranean caves to once again walk the land. The underlings began the ritual after a silent prayer to Akatash, arch-demon of the dead. He was as sinister as Druj was sultry and his ways were often wicked and twisted. He was a creature of perverse design.

They began the incantation and as they continued chanting the face of their victim appeared in the mirrors before them. They waited patiently for their victim to fall asleep, but unlike previous nights, today was different. The hour was close to midnight, the bewitching hour of haunting, but their victim, had not yet fallen asleep. They continued to hone in on their target when they were interrupted by an unexpected disturbance in the mirrors and the images of their victim was suddenly replaced by their own. The High Priestess swore profanely, someone was trying to reverse the spell, and they appeared to be succeeding. "Concentrate" she screamed. "Clear your minds and focus your thoughts", "your lives depend upon it" she yelled frantically.

The underlings started to channel their energies as the image on the mirrors began blurring. They tried desperately to stop the transformation and bring back the image that they sought but whatever was on the other side was much stronger. The High Priestess felt herself weakening, her energies drained by the collective efforts of her underlings. The images on the mirrors started moving around in circular motions when suddenly the underlings caught a true reflection of themselves. They screamed at the hideous, contorted images before them, losing their concentration and the glass in the mirrors shattered into a thousand fragments. From within came a burst of flames which set them alight. They yelled and screamed in anguish as the scorching fires razed their bodies but it was to no avail. Within minutes the underlings were reduced to smoldering ashes. The High Priestess sank to her knees, and buried her face in her hands, beaten.

As Usan made his regular rounds, the events of the night in Gilgit weighed heavily on his mind. It was the first time he had been part of such an unnerving dream and he was still uncertain if it was a dream or if the witch had really been there. So he was relieved to see Nawang ride up to him on his paint stallion kicking up the dust as he did so on a hot summer afternoon. He was glad to see his friend and he was glad for the company. The pair didn't do much but sit back in a local tavern feeling the humid blast of the hot midday sun streaming through the cloudless sky.

They willed the day away, sipping on bottles of cider and exchanging stories instead of doing their customary rounds. Usan decided not to mention anything about his dream and preferred to store it away at the back of his mind. It was close to midnight when they left. Both men were reduced to a stupor from the afternoon escapade and they decided to do the unthinkable, pitch a tent in the middle of nowhere and cook some food when there were perfectly cozy rooms available for rent. No man or woman has yet acted rationally under the influence of alcohol and the pair were no different. Usan started to light the fire after collecting an armful of firewood and Nawang was preparing the mutton. Something about being intoxicated prompted the craving for meat, when he suddenly felt a cold chill run up his spine. He was sober instantly and reached for the hilt of his sword which was strapped to his back. Nawang did the same; they both sensed imminent danger.

———◆✕◆———

Ahriman stood up and looked around. The twelve acolytes who had freed him from his prison sat silently in rows of six on either side of his throne. A smile lit up his face as he thought of the luxuries mortals bestowed upon him. It never once occurred to their feeble minds that as the overlord of darkness he had no need for niceties or pleasantries. Even in the dark realm, he lived far more luxuriously then they could ever imagine. Yet it suited their needs to surround him with unimaginable comforts. Their god could not be seen wanting.

He stood up and paced back and forth. The acolytes who were shrouded in black robes with hoods flung over their heads sat silently, watching, not wanting to distress their master in anyway.

Druj's disciple had failed but he could not take it out on her. She was as eternal as he was.

"Summon the augur" he yelled. The acolytes obeyed and minutes later an old woman, bent almost to the middle made her way into the room, holding a staff in one hand and a crystal ball in the other. She was about to utter the customary greeting but Ahriman cut her off with a wave of his hand. "Tell me old hag of the seven seas, what are the offspring's of Hawk's Nest doing now". The witch sat crossed legged on the red carpeted floor before the throne and placed the crystal ball on the floor in front of her. She rolled her hand lightly over the ball mumbling sacred verses through her toothless mouth and shortly after a mist appeared within the ball. The mist slowly faded away to revealed the whereabouts of Usan and Nawang as they labored around a fire cooking their meal. "They're cooking, my lord" she replied.

Ahriman looked into the crystal ball and the sight of the pair striving away around a fire brought a smirk to his face. Ahriman let out a laugh, Druj's favorite had failed him. "Bring the priestess to me" he commanded, his voice thundering across the room. The acolytes obeyed and within minutes the priestess was brought before him, through an open portal. The High Priestess was pale and the moment she saw him, Ahriman or Angra Mainyu, the very fabric of evil, she dropped to her knees, weeping out aloud, begging for mercy.

<hr />

She looked at herself in the mirror and caught sight of her own reflection. Her smooth pale skin was the color of winter snow; her face was without lines or wrinkles, her lips as red as the petals of a midsummer rose. Her eyes as blue and as deep as the endless ocean, her figure petite and well proportioned. She was almost six feet tall and she made a handsome woman. She remembered a time when she lived in a distant land filled with snowcapped peaks and undulating valleys. She had not been without suitors and many a handsome young man had made his way to her doorstep asking for her hand in marriage but she turned them all down, waiting on perfection. Perfection never came and days soon turned into months and months into years and then one day she looked at herself in the mirror and beside the contour of her eye she saw a tiny crease. Age had caught up with her. She remembered the fear she had felt, the fear of forever being stuck in a valley in the middle of nowhere, not being able to make something of herself.

That's how it started, in front of the accursed mirror. She was drawn to it, she was drawn to herself. She remembered crying in front of the mirror, overwhelmed by the fear of an uneventful life. She felt cheated, deprived of what could have been without anyone to turn to. It was her vanity that had led to this. She felt that no one had listened to her but eventually someone did, the mirror. That night she had a dream, she saw a lady, tall and fair, slim and petite, infinitely prettier than herself. The lady spoke to her in gentle whispers, her words soft and silken, in a tone sweeter than an angel's harp. She was one of the select few who had been fortunate enough see her, the queen, Druj. She was a gentle queen who had taken her into her folds and brought her to her temple, in the middle of a lush green forest. It was here that the queen inducted her into the temple and taught her the secrets of the deceivers. It was the beginning of a new life and hundreds of years would go by before she ever saw the light of day again. It was to this benevolent queen that she turned in her most perilous hour, in her hour of need and in her mind it was her intervention that had saved her. Ahriman had not killed her. Instead he spared her with words of kindness. Clemency from the very personification of evil was something she had not expected and the priestess felt certain that the queen had interceded on her behalf.

The priestess stood in front of the mirror and summoned the queen, uttering the magical verses that would bring her forth, and Druj did not disappoint her. She smiled at her priestess, who had been the first of her kind, and listened patiently as she thanked her. "Thank you most benevolent queen" surmised the High Priestess after minutes of pouring out her gratitude. "Why do you thank me, Anushka, my little lamb?" asked the queen. "Because you saved me, your highness" she replied. "I did not save you little one; it was Ahriman himself who did that. He could see your soul and he knew it was pure. He may be a creature of darkness but he is not unmitigated evil. I knew he'd take kindly to you when I employed you in his service" said the queen.

———◆◆✕◆◆———

Back at their residence in Leh, Usan Holdings had managed to purchase a tavern that they kept exclusively for their staff residence; Karmina was in her study when she suddenly felt the unnerving pangs of danger.

She rushed to the altar that was located in the prayer room at the other end of the tavern, on the upper floor and lit the fire in the sacred altar. Karmina uttered a prayer to Safa the most sapient lord of fire.

"I denounce all evil and carry out this prayer in the name of Safa, the most radiant, luminous and effulgent of all beings. He who is of immaculate conception, he who is firm of mind and spirit, whose purity of soul is never in contention."

"I petition for his guidance as he stands by us in our hour of need. I petition for his assistance and protection as we seek to repel the virulent evil that strives to touch our soul. Aid us Safa, most glorious of beings in our hour of need"

As she repeated the prayers, she looked into the flames, and she could see the effigy of the High Priestesses of Druj. She saw the image of Anushka.

She summoned the goddess, who is the tongue of fire, Kali, she who wore around her neck a garland of a hundred skulls, she who cleaved the head of demons with her double edged sword and she who drained their blood with her vampiric teeth. She who is known as the devourer of time and of all things finite. She petitioned the goddess to reveal in the mirrors, the image of the lookers, which was grotesquely hideous and beyond mortal description.

Rise of a Merchant II

The danger passed within minutes and all traces of alcohol vanished from their system as quickly as it had appeared. Nawang gave Usan a quizzical look as if to say "what was that" and Usan simply shook his head, not knowing what to reply. "I think we should return to Leh as soon as possible" he said and Nawang nodded his head in agreement.

The prepared a quick meal, frying the sliced meat in a pan on a scintillating fire, after adding luxuriant drops of olive oil to it, without taking the trouble to marinate the meat. The thinly cut stakes sizzled in the hot oil and were ready within twenty minutes. They dug in, and the fried mutton was rather tasty. Usan realized that it was the fat in the meat that gave it, its natural flavor and it tasted succulent even without added herbs or spices.

They slept on thick blankets which they had strewn on the ground and dozed off without giving much thought to the events that had transpired. They woke up at sunset and made a quick breakfast of the leftovers from the previous night before they saddled their horses and rode on.

It was another four days to Leh and the pair didn't overly push the pace stopping at regular intervals for food and rest in the villages and the towns that they passed. It was at sundown on the fourth day that they reached the outskirts of Leh. The town hadn't changed much in five years. With the exception of the changing seasons, it remained the same.

The proprietors of Usan Holdings took a special interest in the town, and Usan personally had a hand in its continued development. It was one of the few accolades that he could take credit for.

The volume of correspondence between Usan Holdings and Hawk's Nest had also increased in that time and the company had a special batch of riders on standby to ferry regular messages to and from Hawk's Nest. Most of the messages were coded in cuneiform and it was deciphered by the office of Amesha Spenta and disseminated accordingly among those who were privy to the information.

They rode towards the rear of the tavern where the team had a stable. The young attendant Yeshe who was now in charge of all the stables that belonged to Usan Holdings, a duty that carried with it grave and onerous responsibilities given the number of horses that the stables managed, was there to greet them.

Yeshe was normally away but the fates had conspired on this particular day to bring the young man home and he was at hand to meet Nawang and Usan. He smiled as the pair rode in and Usan nodded his head in acknowledgment.

Yeshe was now completely indoctrinated in the philosophy of Hawk's Nest and was becoming quite astute at gathering information.

He had managed to build an extensive network with the help of other stable hands, who supplied him with information on visitors who frequented their stables, especially strangers, for a nominal sum of course. Not that all the information that he gathered was accurate but that was beside the point. It was left to Usan and Karmina to filter through all the bits of information that came their way and decide what was relevant and what was not.

They had a quick chat before Usan headed for the backdoor of the tavern with Nawang following close behind. Without realizing it he had acquired the feel for leadership and had gradually eased into it. His position in the Chamber of Commerce had helped him immensely, and he was no longer averse to speaking in front of large crowds. His ability to watch and listen had helped him gain the confidence that he needed, if not to put forward his own ideas than at the very least to emulate that of others. He hadn't yet developed his own style but that would come in time. He was exuberant when it came to matters of religion but was diffident when it came to matters of commerce. Fortunately Dechen was on hand to devote many painstaking hours in his pursuit to achieve the higher goal that he so earnestly desired, which was of course to be the master spy.

The thought of becoming the most vaunted agent in Hawk's Nest inspired him no end. He worked in secret to achieve his one true aspiration in life and in the pursuit of glory; all thoughts of women fell to the wayside, well temporarily at least.

The back room of the tavern led to the kitchen which was adjoined to the dining room. Only a thin wall separated the both. He made his way to the main tavern which was now converted into an office and as per the norm he found Karmina seated behind a chair, shuffling through a stack of papers. Nawang in the meantime headed up the staircase located at the opposite end of the dining quarters and made his way to his well-furnished, if slightly untidy room.

Karmina looked up as she saw her brother enter and she greeted him with a smile, warm, natural and pleasant. It occurred to him that his sister had unusually white teeth but he decided to let the thought slip given the gravity of the situation and question he was about to pose. She pointed to a seat and just as he slumped into it and opened his mouth to say something, she said "Ahriman" in anticipation to the well-structured and politely phrased question that never left his lips.

Usan knew it was pointless but he asked anyway "How did you know?". "I know everything little brother, who do you think saved you after your drinking binge with Nawang?" she asked. Usan looked resigned. "So he's back" he added feebly. Karmina nodded.

Ahriman was the eternal spirit of evil and during the battle before time the forces of good had gathered under

Ahura Mazda and the forces of evil had gathered under Ahriman. Druj the goddess of lies and deceit was his principle lieutenant. Following the defeat of the forces of darkness, the demon legions were relegated to the abyss and the guardship of the prison was handed to the keeper of the abyss who himself was a somewhat dubious personality. In the time that had gone by since the earth shattering battle he had managed to open the gates of the abyss to let a demon or two slip away.

Following the defeat Ahriman went into self-imposed exile and relegated himself to a world of his own made accessible only by a portal that was known to the most potent wizards. He had construed a paradise for himself. He did return a few thousand years after the mammoth battle to the Central Kingdoms that were his bastion but according to all reports he had tired of the world of mortals. Only someone who was important to him and could have made him come back and all evidence pointed to a close nexus between Ahriman and the Dark Lord.

"I must be coming a thorn on his side" said Usan. Karmina nodded her head "we can be assured of more attacks" she said.

———◆◆)◆(◆◆———

The banquet hall was a grand place. The huge mahogany table in the middle took up most of the space in the dark romantic room. Left without a tablecloth and daring guests to tarnish its perfectly varnished shine with imprints from their fingers, it stood its ground boldly. Two tall silver candelabras stood silently like lighthouses on a moonless night guiding the guests to the center of the table and the room was brought to life by the scented fragrance that the candles emitted.

It was the first time that they had been together in months and the initial team of Usan, Karmina, Sonum, Nima, Dechen, Dorjee, Nawang, Yeshe and Kalden decided that it was occasion enough for them to celebrate. Despite the formal attire and the solemn atmosphere the assembly dispensed with formalities and chirped away like larks.

The real star of the night was however the food. The table was lined with platters of food served on rare silverware. Roast mutton, barbequed venison, boneless chicken drizzled in sauces or begging to be dipped in spicy concoctions, paved the way towards a scrumptious dinner. Countless cheeses, breads, vegetables, sweets, and bottles of delectable red wine enhanced the repertoire.

The company feasted to their hearts content. The conversation was light and festive and they spent their time indulging in the food and wine that was on display. The party continued until midnight before the crowd dispersed. After a splendid night of merriment they headed for bed.

———◆◆◆◆◆———

Anushka wore a black clock, the purple streak above her forehead stood out in the light of the blood moon. She was escorted by two young maidens no older than sixteen the color of their hair as dazzling as the rays of the golden sun and their emerald green eyes were devoid of emotion. She drew a five pointed star on the ground, with the help of her attendants followed by a circle that connected the triangular tips of the stars together. At each of the five tips her attendants placed a long candle that was lighted while Anushka passed around a slice of black turnip and each of them had a bite. She then lifted a skull from the satchel that was slung across her shoulders and filled it with the dense red liquid that she had stored in a bottle. Once the hollow of the skull was filled to the brim, she lifted the skull up towards the moon and murmured "Hail Druj, sultry, sybaritic Venus, who ensnares men with passionate dreams, her curvaceous body provoking every fiber in their body, intoxicating them with her charms, rousing them with dreams beyond mortal comprehension." "Hail the maiden who is untouched and undefiled by mortal hands, whose skin is as soft as the petals of a midsummer rose, her soft, succulent lips tempting the hearts of all men, her eyes the color of green emeralds, deep and intense, radiant and luxuriant"

Druj was a goddess who was pleased by flattery and unlike most conventional goddesses, who preferred lines from a sacred text, Druj preferred her worshippers to make sensual inferences to her and such connotations caught her instant attention. Anushka was one of her favorites and the Goddess was easily pleased by her salutations. The circle in the center glowed and the lady who was almost as sultry as the goddess she worshipped, intoxicated by the blood that she had consumed walked over to the center of the circle, her hips swaying in rhythmic fashion as she moved and lay flat in the middle. She started chanting repeatedly. "Goddess shield goddess guide, goddess light the blinding night. Goddess take me in you stride to haunt the dreams of he who is in my sight. Make him cower make him cringe, let me fill his dreams with fright". She kept repeating the lines over and over again, her eyelids getting heavier with each passing minute until she eventually found herself walking in a meadow.

It was filled with tall grass, uniform in its contour, swaying only to the gush of the occasional wind. The wild flowers were a cacophony of colors ranging from fading green grass, purple thistles, blue cornflowers, red poppies and tall asters with yellow centers.

The trail led to a barn painted with the color of unfinished wood, weathered by countless years of being exposed to the elements and baked to a crisp by the hot summer sun. The wood itself was cracked, warped and twisted betraying signs of wear and tear.

Inside she found Usan lying on a bundle of golden hay, in deep slumber, wearing the loose fitting robes of a monk, the soft light glancing off his shaven head. He appeared to be in deep prophet like meditation, which was not unlike Usan, but in reality he was fast asleep after a heavy meal.

Anushka silently inched closer, her hands flushing out a double edged dagger, with a long menacing blade that was tucked beneath her long flowing purple robes, its fabric patterned with dark flowers, until her hand was just above his chest. She uttered a prayer to Druj and drove the dagger down, as hard as she could when suddenly a hand reached out from nowhere to grab her wrist.

Anushka was caught off guard and instinctively resisted the attempt to thwart her attack but Usan who had awakened just at the right time continued to fight off the attack. The struggle that ensued in the dream like state was as sapping if not more exhausting than any in real life. Usan exerted all the energy he could muster while the rest of his body went limp as Anushka kept plunging the dagger into his chest. The struggle continued until the crow of a rooster rang out from nowhere and the apparition disappeared without a trace. Usan opened his eyes to realize that the sheets beneath his body were drenched with sweat.

He was sapped and sagged, dehydrated to the bone, the life almost drained out of him. He could have been killed by either the dagger or as a result of the struggle and he was fortunate to escape with his life intact. Devote and sincere worship had spared him. It was the single outstanding factor that had saved him.

He dragged himself out of bed, almost falling over as he stood up. He desperately needed a drink but there was not a drop in sight. He wavered and faltered as he made his way to the door, stumbling, almost falling on numerous occasions.

He eventually reached the door and held his hand out to turn the golden knob with barely enough energy to twist it. With the last ounce of strength that remained in him, he turned the knob and he stumbled across the doorway, falling. Fortunately Dorjee was walking along the corridor and held out his arms in the nick of time to stop Usan from landing on the carpeted floor.

He lifted the young man; the former herder was blessed with the strength of an ox and carried him to Karmina's office where he laid him down gently on a soft velvet couch. Karmina who was sifting through some papers, the noted archeress was reduced to being a bit of a paper shuffler in recent times, walked over and knelt gently by her brother's side.

She placed her hand on his forehead and rubbed it nimbly with her palms, "Witchcraft" she whispered softly. "Let him rest, while I send word to Hawk's Nest".

Fortunately the rider didn't have to make the whole journey on his own. He rode to the nearest dispatch center, which was normally a small inconspicuous stable stationed in the outskirts of a town or a village that had a rider and fresh horses on standby.

Most visitors wouldn't suspect a thing, taking the station as another run of the mill stable. The stables were constructed in a manner that wouldn't stand out or be noticeable, to blend in with the surroundings, and normally attracted very little attention. They were transit points for riders who ferried messages to and from Hawk's Nest.

It was almost a fortnight before help from Hawk's Nest arrived in the form of a healer whose name was Aashritha. She was ushered in, as soon as she arrived, to see Karmina, by Dorjee and Nawang, who were concerned for the safety and wellbeing of their friend. Usan had been drifting in and out of sleep since the incident, and had both paled and thinned considerably. He had been bedridden for the duration of the time and had been hand fed by either Karmina, Sonum, or Dechen. Aashritha gave him a quick examination and delivered her prognosis "He is without doubt a victim of black magic" she concluded. "The attack was twofold, that which was visible and that which was subtle. The latter attack has caused the sugar in his blood to remain clotted and blocked it from getting into his cells. The sugar remains undiluted in his system" "Hence the cells do not receive any sugar for energy and they begin to breakdown body fat and muscle tissue for energy" "That is the reason why he has thinned and remains listless" she continued. Karmina looked concerned "Is it serious" she asked. "Very" replied Aashritha. "If I had arrived a couple of days later, he would have been a goner for sure" she continued. "Tell me" she inquired did he have any dreams" Karmina nodded her head. "He dreamt of a woman with a dagger" she said and went on to describe the dream to Aashrita, telling her everything she had managed to discern from Usan. The healer listened keenly to what the archeress had to say.

Rise of a Merchant III

It took Usan almost a fortnight to recover from his illness. Ashritha managed to concoct a potion for him made from rare herbs that grew in the concealed crevices of the Kush Mountains to reverse the effects of the attack. He had to take regular intakes of the potion. It was a thick paste that tasted bitter and in addition to helping deliver sugar to the cells, it also absorbed the extra sugar in his bloodstream.

His diet was reduced to chicken broth with slices of salted fish or lamb and regular intakes of his medication which he had to consume just before his meals. Usan remained indisposed for almost a month and Karmina feared that in that time he might forget all the skills and training that he acquired at Hawk's Nest but Ashritha assured her that her fears were unfounded and it was only a matter of time before he returned to his normal self.

"I'm concerned about the attacks" said Karmina to Ashritha, when they had the time to discuss the situation. "I think it is a simple matter of an attempted assassination" the healer responded. "Assassins operate in different ways and not all of them stoop to a knife in the back on a dark night" said Ashrita.

"The attack is done when the victim is asleep by invading his or her dreams. Often the victim is reduce to a state of sheer ecstasy and he is deprived of all his senses. There are some signs that would let the victim know that his dreams were being invaded but he has to know what to look out for."

"For example, he would feel as if he was falling into an endless pit or he could feel that his bed was rocking or gently swaying on the surface of a sea".

"There are normally two types of dream experiences that are distinguishable from each other. The first is the spiritual experience, where the dreamer feels his spirit drifting higher towards the clouds or his soul scaling a shaman tree. The former dreams of ascension allow the soul to expand and form a direct link with the Brahmatma. The latter dreams are dreams of invasion or dreams of regression that puts the dreamer at the mercy of the negative aspect of the super soul" "There is in addition a third category of dreams which is available only to those who embody the qualities of Amesha Spenta, where they can descend to the world of the dead and speak to spirits of those who have perished"

Karmina nodded her head. Anyone gifted with the talent understood the dualistic nature of existence. Both good and evil originated from the same source, there was but the one ultimate source to all things. At the beginning of time, in the mortal perception of time, the source split into two distinct entities, one good and the other evil. The struggle between them is constant and perpetual.

"Do you know the type of magic that was used?" she asked and Ashrita nodded her head. It was the magic of Druj, the highest ranking member of the circle of Ahriman.

"The corpses of all men is infested by the spirit of Druj and hence infested with lies and deceit. Corpses are cremated or left as vulture feed so that the essence of lies and deceit cannot defile the earth"

"In the beginning all corpses were required to be cremated but following the untold deaths in the battle before time where many bodies were left un-cremated on the numerous battlefields across the mortal plane, corpses that were fed on by vultures were deemed to be given a suitable burial in accordance with the eternal laws of the Brahmatma. The vulture once it ingests and digests the remains of the carcass absorbs the essence of Druj into its being where it remains trapped" she explained.

"Druj presides over the city of Necroplis or the city of the dead. At the entrance to the city there is a large statute erected in honor of the Goddess, with the head of a vulture sitting prettily on her shoulders. She wears a polished circlet around her head, studded with diamonds" "She is also known as the white goddess because her skin is as pale and as untouched as fresh snow."

"The city is located in the middle of harsh inhospitable desert, an oasis in the midst of nowhere. Its main street is paved with rectangular mud baked houses of identical dimensions lined side by side"

"Each house has a door and each door is a portal to another world. The emissaries of Druj ferried themselves from one world to another through these doors. Only they know its secrets" she continued.

"What of the assassin, are there any clues as to her identity?" asked Karmina. Ashritha shook her head. "All I can tell you is that the cult of Druj is closely associated to Ahriman" "I would suspect that the assassin was a high ranking member of the cult. There were rumors that her cult existed long ago but after Ahriman tired of the world of mortals, little was heard of them and they vanished without a trace for eons until the arrival of the Dark Lord"

"Druj is associated with the planet Venus and unmatched and unparalleled in both wit and beauty. She is captivating, enchanting and mesmerizing. According to ancient legends she has remained pure and untainted by the touch of men from the day of her seismic conception. Her high priestesses like her are beauty personified and therefore it was possible to surmise that whoever the assassin was, she was of unspeakable beauty". Karmina remained silent.

"How do we dispose of the threat?" she asked her eyes ablaze with anger at she thought of the suffering her brother had been put through. "I'm not sure" said Ashritha, we have to locate her whereabouts first and that could be anywhere in the known world."

In the weeks that followed Hawk's Nest had riders dispatched to all corners of the known world to locate the whereabouts of Anushka. It was treated as a matter of utmost urgency. A new evil had surfaced and given the mode of the attempted assassination, many other lives could be in peril if the priestess of Druj was allowed to continue.

It was Sonum that eventually made the decisive breakthrough. She accessed the collective memory of the Sisterhood and had managed to replay images of the ancient Temple of Druj that was stored in their memories. It was a citadel that was located in the middle of an isolate forest. Sonum withdrew into a deep meditative state and the visions that appeared in her mind were as the sisters before her had seen them. It was a ritual that was best attempted at night, given the serenity of the hour.

Sonum started by summoning Tiara, principle deity of the Alchemic Sisterhood. "O Tiara my soul belongs to thee. O my heart from different ages, may there be nothing to hamper my way and may there be no opposition to me from my sisters. May there be no parting of you, Tiara from me, in this journey that I undertake. You are the spirit within my body which strengthens my limbs and guides me on my journey. May you take me forth to the place which I wish to go"

She closed her eyes and felt herself drifting back in time, down the ages, to a place that was distant and long forgotten. The structure that she saw before her was three stories high. The walls were of varying thickness. Around the structure were a series of chambers of different sizes. There were windows on the temple walls with fixed latticework. The largest and the most ornamented chamber was that of the High Priestess. The interior of the chamber was lined with cedar and overlaid with pure gold. The chamber of the High Priestess contained two statues of Druj, each ten cubits high, adorned with an armor of blazing gold inlaid with precious stones. A veil of variegated linen covered the entrance to the chamber of the High Priestess.

The other chambers were smaller and identical in dimensions. The walls were lined with cedar, on which were carved figurines of the goddess decorated with sculptured palm trees and ornamented with flowers which were covered with gold.

The floor of the temple was made of fir and it was carpeted with gold, polished and refined. The doors and posts that held the temple together were made of oak. On both sides of the doors were hand crafted statues of Druj, shaped from the rarest wood.

Within the chamber of the High Priestess, there was an additional chamber, constructed for the underlings and within this chamber there were twelve mirrors on a table similar to a household dressing table with a velvet seat in front of each table. The tables were arranged in a circle.

Erected in the center of the circle of tables with mirrors, was a little cubicle made of the rarest cedar, held on three sides by walled cedar and a door that slid to the left on the fourth side. The wood was polished to perfection and there were intricate carvings on all walls, depicting Druj naked to the waist, her junoesque body surpassing that of any mortal woman. There were scattered bits of glass strewn on the floor, a dead giveaway that this was indeed that the temple that had been used for the attack. The fragments of glass that were visible were from the mirrors that had shattered from Karmina's unexpected and unpremeditated response.

Sonum had seen enough, and brought her consciousness back to the present, drifting back to normal in slow well timed intervals. Once she had regained her composure and had returned to normality, she made her way to the staff meeting quarters, which was an informal meeting place for members of Usan Holdings to meet, congregate and exchange ideas. She smiled when she saw a rather feeble Usan, seated on a chair, talking to Nima. He looked thin and pale, almost frail, like he had been beaten down with a carpet beater and hung out to dry. She couldn't help but feel sorry for the young man.

She reported her findings to the archeress and Karmina didn't waste any time. She immediately discussed the matter with the rest of the team. The final outcome was the obvious; they had to neutralize the evil that lurked within the temple walls.

Sonum mapped out a route to the temple from memory. It was located in Rutania, an isolated kingdom in the vast region that was known as the outlands.

The outlands were a region to the west of the former empire located between the former empire and the Central Kingdoms. It made sense. It was a virtually unknown region and its proximity to both the former empire and the Central Kingdoms made it ideal for use as a base of operations for any strikes against kingdoms of the former empire.

It the older days when trade was feasible between the Central Kingdoms and the Empire, merchants traversed the region but since the fall of the Empire, its former kingdoms had banded together and chose instead to foster trade between them and to opt out of any formal arrangements with the outlands. It was partly economical and partly due to the setbacks that the Empire had suffered in the days prior to its decline. Given the current situation it was essential that Hawk's Nest gained a firm foothold in the outlands.

The temple was constructed in the middle of a forest that was once teeming with life but in the years that had gone by most of its natural occupants had fallen victim to the horrors that now occupied it. The trees that had sheltered so many with their spreading canopy of green were no longer vibrant and the leaves only fluttered to the squall of unholy wind. Neither insect nor animal could prosper or prospect here.

------◆◆◆◆◆------

Anushka looked at the aberration on her wrist. Despite the weeks that had passed by the scar remained unhealed. It was like she was wearing a red armband. The grip was strong and brutal and the imprint it left on her hand would not disappear despite all her efforts. She had tried every spell she knew and even performed a minor blood sacrifice in honor of Druj. The goddess herself had appeared in her most auspicious form to try to appease her aggrieved disciple but it was to no avail.

Ahriman had ordered the execution and no doubt he would be displeased. Surprisingly he hadn't said anything as of yet but Ahriman worked in ways known only to himself. A sudden thought struck her; maybe it was her death that he wanted, retribution for her failure. She dismissed it after a minute or two deciding that Ahriman could have easily destroyed her if he wanted to and he didn't need to resort to any other means to do so.

She had hired the services of a paid assassin, the best in the business she was told, to make a hit on the day when Usan left the meeting at the Chamber of Commerce, but the assassin had blundered and the alert merchant had escaped. It was left to her to orchestrate his demise but her attempts had been so savagely routed that she hesitated to try again.

Druj appeared to console her favorite, "Calm down, child" she urged. "Get a grip on yourself". The goddess brushed the tears off Anuska's eyes with her hands. The maiden was averse to failure and the word to her was a perverse curse. She had remained faithful to Druj since the fateful night when she had sat in front of a mirror and wished that her beauty would remain as eternal as time itself. She looked at the mirror again and she looked the same as she had hundreds of years ago. Despite the passing of the years she had remained faithful in the service of the goddess and

Druj, Venus herself, had blessed her. "O Venus beauty of the skies, whose eyes speak of a thousand smiles. O goddess of infinite grace and unrivalled beauty, benevolent in touch and propitious in embrace, guide your lamb like a shepherd does his flock on to the path of victory". Druj heard her laments and was lost in gentle thought. She was moved by Anushka's pleas.

The goddess felt her iron will faltering, and her nerves of steel ailing. She decided magnanimously to ease her burden and to let nature take its cause.

Rise of a Merchant IV

They did waste too much time and set off to locate the temple as soon as they could, travelling with the barest minimum. The road Sonum had mapped out took them through the Kingdom of Rowina and once they had reached the city of Halla in the northernmost province of Farahan, they had to veer left, and steer across the Jarahi River before heading towards Saratonia, a minor landlocked agricultural kingdom. The route took them through vast wooden plains, intersected by numerous valleys that formed a part of the Zarnia mountain system. It was a pastoral land and many of its inhabitants were farmers who were occupied in the lush green fields that had been cleared for grazing. It was the first time any of them had ventured into the outlands but many of the former members of the Serf Guard had made their homes here, following the informal peace that persisted in Rowina. The kingdom looked more stable than many suspected.

Jedzimir had sent word ahead of their arrival and they had a young guide, who was waiting to show them the way. He was a pleasant looking lad no older than sixteen whose parents had retired from provisional duties. The couple ran a farmstead by day and ferried arms across the border by night.

The boy's name was Vlad. He was raised in the country and was well versed with the forest tracks that were commonly used for smuggling. It was a lucrative enterprise in these parts and the authorities often closed an eye, preferring instead to have a share in the cake. The outlands were landlocked between the two warring armies and hence in an ideal position to reap the rewards from the ongoing conflict. Vlad was a jovial lad who had a cheerful outlook on life and got along well with almost everyone. He rode in the lead with Nawang and together the pair helped the others blaze away. The air was alive with the smell of fresh wet grass and as they rode by they could see pastures on either side with cows leisurely grazing away. The tracks were not well maintained and Nawang and Vlad had to keep an eye out for ruts, pot holes, rabbit warrens and stones that were partially hidden in the long meadow grass.

Usan shook his head ruefully as they whizzed past Saratonia taking in as much as he could. When things were better he hoped to expand and the outlands looked prime for the picking.

They passed the odd monastery that was erected by the more adventurous missionary to further the teachings and the reach of the religious order but the extent of their influence remained doubtful. They managed to cross Saratonia within a week where they said goodbye to their young escort and ventured into more densely forested territories, before reaching the outskirts of Rutania.

"They're coming, they're coming" whispered a soft voice and Anushka awoke from sleep. She dressed and walked out of her chamber into the wide open space of the temple courtyard. The temple lay like an old fortress, the moonlight shinning off its craggy, facade with moss clinging to the shade of the ancient walls.

An ominous silence hung gingerly in the air. She paused and all that she could hear was the susurration of the leaves in the ghostly wind. Looking up, she stared transfixed at the myriad of fluttering shapes that danced in the high boughs, almost hypnotized, but the longer she stared the more the leaves looked like eyes that were staring back. She paced up and down thinking, pondering and reassessing the situation. She summoned the keeper of the temple. "Raise the alarm" she ordered.

———◆◆✕◆●———

"There" said Nawang. He raised his right hand and pointed towards the top of a forlorn hill. Karmina looked up and saw a figure on a black horse, clad in an outfit as dark as a funeral scarf, the face semi covered with only the eyes visible. The cloaked rider had a sword strapped to the side that was clearly visible in the light of day. "That's an assassin" said Karmina silently. Nawang nodded his head while Nima stepped up to take closer order.

Their watcher was evidently female, a detail that was made conspicuous by the strands of long black hair that fell well below her shoulders, dancing gently to the breeze that drifted in from the south.

"She's no slouch" said the maiden from Tarchem. "In fact I'd say she's deadly". She paused for a minute before she continued. "Maybe we should have brought a battalion of knights with us". Karmina shook her head. "That wouldn't have been wise. These are independent territories and an army riding through would only invite reprisals from the Dark Lord" she said. "It might give him an excuse to intervene and escalate the war and that is something that we don't want or need at the moment". Nima nodded her head. "She is just watching us for now anyway" she said. "It looks like she is going to trail us" said Nawang with a shrug of his shoulders. "We are strangers in her territory. She has the advantage and I'm certain that there are others with her. They are going to wait for the right moment before they strike" he said not sounding overly perturbed. It was a bit too late to worry about things and they had to face whatever came their way.

"Let's move on" she Karmina and they continued at a more subdued pace, keeping their eyes on the mysterious rider seated on the back of a black stallion. Karmina kept turning back to see if Usan was well. The young man didn't at all look out of sorts.

As a matter of fact he was lost in thought. Something about his assassin had touched him and when she plunged the dagger into his chest, he couldn't but help look into her eyes. He saw apprehension and felt the trepidation that was haunting her. It wasn't hate or anger that drove her to the verge of killing him, it was something else, something entirely different. It was fear; perhaps it was the fear of failure.

He thought that she was pretty, the prettiest woman he had seen yet. He felt her skin when she touched him; it was soft and silken, smooth and unwavering, sensuous and unblemished. It aroused feelings within him that he could not explain. He was suddenly overcome by a bout of unexplained sadness and he felt tears well up in his eyes.

They reached Ruthania without too much fuss. It was a densely forested country, with trees that were hundreds if not thousands of years old. The leaves formed a natural awning that blocked the sun from filtering through and there was almost little or no undergrowth. It was difficult to find open patches unless the trees had been cleared for farming, which was the case in many areas. They stumbled on patches of empty land or abandoned farms which made for the ideal camping site. It was a kingdom that held many secrets and outsiders had little or no knowledge of its intricacies. Even the extensive network of spies and informers employed by Hawk's Nest had little knowledge of the kingdom. Most of what they knew was from the memory archives of the Sisterhood.

As they journeyed through the fertile land filled with trees that displayed the luminescent shades of green, yellow and orange, dotting the countryside, they stumbled on to a clearing with a little hill on the horizon and a small fresh water creek running through it. It looked like the perfect place to pitch a tent. They unpacked their gear and sheltered by the creek, lighting a fire that could be spotted from miles away. It was pointless taking any precautions and to anyone who looked on it appeared like they were having a party. Despite the festive facade the mood in the camp was somber.

They were doing the unthinkable, taking on an enemy that was many times their size on a terrain that was relatively unknown. It was enough to give anyone sleepless nights, let alone a company of seven who were desperately trying to save someone they loved.

Nima woke up at the light of dawn and she was the first to spot them. She let out a little gasp that brought the others instantly to their feet. They looked up to where she was looking and they saw twelve riders astride twelve black stallions, all almost equal in height, tall and leathery, smog flaring from their nostrils with the rising sun to their backs. There was a thirteenth rider who rode slightly ahead of the rest who was none other than their overt shadow.

It was a clear, concise, unmistakable message. They put on their armor quietly, slipping into their mail shirts and readied their weapons before they clambered on to their horses and prepared to meet the onslaught. Karmina took the lead with Nawang, Dorjee, Usan, Sonum, Nima and Aashrita in the middle. Dechen was relegated to the rear. She was the least trained in battle and without doubt would be the first to falter. Under normal circumstances she would have been spared the fighting but it was a day when no such privileges could be conferred. She was confined to the rear and equipped with a longbow. Her orders were to fire volley after volley until the enemy was defeated or she fell, whichever came first.

The sun slowly rose higher and it revealed a brilliant shine that glistened off the shimmering armor of the thirteen riders. Their armor was polished to elegance, oozing finesse that was beyond mortal ability. They stood facing each other and their opponents watched giving Karmina and the others time to ready themselves. Maybe they were giving them the option to surrender, no one could tell. When they were convinced that Karmina and the others were battle ready their leader reached for the hilt of the sword that she had strapped to her side and lifted the blade clear from its sheath. She held it high pointing it towards the sky and looked up upwards murmuring a silent prayer before she let her head drop and pointed the sword directly at them.

Anushka gave the signal and the horses moved forward, their hoofs beating in unison as they thundered on the ground. "Ready" yelled Karmina and the team lifted their bows in preparation. Karmina aimed her arrow at Anushka, the leader of the pack, and waited until she was within striking distance. "Wait, wait" she cried out, patiently waiting for the enemy to get within striking distance. When she was certain that the arrows would not go astray, she yelled out a decisive "now" and they let the arrows rip. The shaft that was aimed at Anushka flew swiftly through the air but just as it was about to pierce her skin, she fended in off with her sword and the arrow fizzled away harmlessly landing tamely on the ground. Karmina looked surprised.

The others didn't have much luck either. Some of the arrows hit their target but they bounced harmlessly away barely denting the armor of the acolytes.

Karmina and the others dropped their bows and drew their swords. The acolytes were upon them like a flash, their swords sweeping right and left in the manner of trained swordsmen. Outnumbered it was a desperate fight and the team were losing ground within seconds. Karmina hoped to take on Anushka but the High Priestess ignored her and headed directly for Usan who just managed to do enough to avoid a suave stroke aimed at his ribs.

He deflected it with his blade and as soon as the swords clashed he knew it was a halfhearted stroke that was directed without the usual force or brutality. It was done more to scare or injure than to kill and he was surprised. He retaliated with a wild counter stroke that appeared to be more of a face saving maneuver than anything else. He sensed a faint giggle and he tried to suppress a laugh. A conflict of wills often released unquantifiable energy and the meeting of opposing forces sometimes resulted in a positive outcome.

They would have been cut to pieces by the sheer savagery of the acolytes if it wasn't for the sudden blaze of trumpets that heralded the arrival of the Ruby Knights, the third highest military order in Hawk's Nest. From the trees beyond the clearing there was a rush of horses, and the man in the lead, the grandmaster was none other than Triloka himself, the once renegade general who was like a father to Usan and Karmina.

The acolytes turned to meet the new threat. Their neither faltered nor retreated. Instead they readjusted their positions to meet the enemy, ignoring Karmina and the others, while

Usan and Anushka busied themselves with their own private war. The lead knight whose eyes were the color of bronze took charge of proceedings. Karmina brought her sword to her face, to grant the enemy the honor that were granted prior to battle. The acolytes regrouped in formation and waited for the newcomers to come within the required distance. As they did so the knight with the bronze eyes moved forward to position his horse slightly ahead of the rest. He discarded the black robes that concealed his body to reveal a man clad in glistening black armor that sparkled in the light of the morning sun. His skin like the color of his eyes was a darkened bronze and when he spoke his voice was like that of brazen thunder, deep and ominous. "I'm Gilgamesh, chief preceptor of the Temple of Ahriman" he said.

The sound of his voice brought the fighting to a standstill. Usan let his sword drop in meek cognizance, awed by the presence of the greatest warrior to ever grace the face of the earth.

"I'm Triloka of the Ruby Knights" responded the grandmaster. Gilgamesh smiled and bowed his head in respect. "Well met grandmaster" he said. Triloka responded with a similar gesture and channeled his energies to the task ahead. He drew his sword from its sheath and as he did so Gilgamesh ordered the charge.

Within minutes the sound of clashing steel rung out across the meadow. It was a battle of sheer brutality, a battle of wit, skill, strength and temperament that epitomized war from all aspects. Anger, fury and passion fueled the raging battle.

The fought like warriors of the highest caliber, which they no doubt were.

Gilgamesh and Triloka faced each other and as the battle progressed the odds began to favor Gilgamesh for Triloka was mortal and like all men he soon began to tire. It wasn't a question of skill but of endurance and Gilgamesh had endured more than any mortal could ever perceive.

The Knights of the Ruby order were all veterans, who had been elevated from the ranks of the Emerald Order for skill not only with the sword but for their ability to command but despite their proven capabilities and their superior numbers, it was obvious that the knights were no match for the acolytes, and while many of the knights were mercifully spared some were cut down ruthlessly, cleaved and hacked to shreds by opponents who were more skilled than them.

Eventually Gilgamesh eased up, feeling sorry for Triloka and not wanting to diminish his status in any way, he lifted his sword to his face and said "till we meet again, grandmaster". He signaled a withdrawal and the acolytes turned their horses and sped away, leaving Anuska behind.

The knights banded together and collected the bodies of their fallen comrades to grant them the burial that they deserved. The gathered wood from the nearby forest, and after bathing and cleaning the wounds of the dead, the bodies were cremated and accorded the appropriate funeral rites.

Epilogue

In the year that followed Anushka was formally inducted into the team and soon became an integral member of Usan Holdings. She filled them in on the acolytes who were in actuality the twelve greatest warriors to grace the face of the known world. Ahriman had freed them from the palace of Ereshkigal, in Irkalla, where they were consigned after death and made them knights of his temple. Gilgamesh, the chief preceptor was accorded the highest honor.

Anushka remained the High Priestess who was faithful to Druj and the Goddess continued to stay by her side. Usan was taken in by her and was soon imprisoned by her hypnotic charm. The captive became the captor and a bewitched Usan finally proposed. Anushka accepted gracefully and the couple were wed with the blessings of the God King, Amesha Spenta.

It was a day of great celebration and there was much merriment following the exchange of marital vows that were affirmed in front of a sacred fire the enduring flame of Safa. The flame enforced the will of Asha the inseparable quality of all celestial and heavenly beings.

It is the responsibility of all men to seek the path of righteousness and should they falter they need only to look towards the unyielding flame that shines like a beacon in the dark, to guide their way. The eternal fire is the spark that enlightens us all and marital vows that are consecrated in the presence of the undying flame endure the test of time.

In the following year Usan Holdings expanded their operations into the outlands under their new subsidiary Anushka Limited by acquiring interests in farms in Saratonia. The new company focused primarily on the sales and exports of dairy products, animal feeds and farm implements. Its mode of operation was slightly different from that of normal trading firms. It deployed a barter system and goods were exchanged for other goods of similar value without a need for the physical transfer of money. It was a mechanism that was adopted to avert corruption and curb inflation by ensuring price stability which in the long run facilitated economic growth.

By avoiding unexpected price hikes or sudden drops in prices, farmers and other enterprises were able to contract and transact with each other with more certainty. It was part of an overall ploy devised by Hawk's Nest and Usan Holdings to bring Saratonia up to scratch.

The situation in Lamunia had taken a turn for the worse, and the fighting continued without respite. The Emerald Knights might have been routed if it hadn't been for the unexpected change in the weather. The winter had been colder than usual that year and temperatures fell well below freezing point.

The harsh weather had many of the enemy troops literally freezing to death in the soles of their shoes. This coupled with a poor harvest had caused a severe shortage of food that was precipitated by the unusually cold conditions just prior to the setting in of winter. Crops withered and perished prematurely. The situation was just as bad for horses. Grazing along the tracks or in meadows was no longer adequate and the condition of the horses deteriorated considerably. Their food had to be supplemented with fodder and supplies were low.

Soon the grass thinned out and animals that brought up the rear of the column fared the worse. Within the first winter month almost ten thousand horses had perished. Their riders were weakened by poor diets, inconsistent rations and were susceptible to fatigue and disease.

It was a scene where tens of thousands of men huddled together and thus contaminated the waterways contributing to a major outbreak of intestinal ailments. The problem compounded as they went deeper into Lamunia.

Allowing the enemy to approach unhindered, the Emerald Knights withdrew further south where the conditions were warmer and the invaders were caught in the middle of ice, sleet and snow which only served to hasten their demise. The retreating knights further set alight farms and poisoned wells making in almost impossible for the enemy to subsist. Despite the intolerable conditions, the armies of the Dark Lord persisted and salvaged what they could. They reserved what they had left for an all-out assault in the coming summer.

Printed in the United States
By Bookmasters